SELF-MADE MILLIONAIRES

Devastating, dark-hearted and…
looking for Brides

From the lowliest slums
to Millionaires' Row…
Through sheer determination
and passionate belief these gorgeous men
have reached the top. They never rested
on their laurels, never relied on fancy
qualifications or inherited cash—
they've fought for every penny they have.

With names synonymous with money,
power and success, these men have everything
now but their brides—and they'll settle for
nothing less than the best!

Self-Made Millionaires **is the**
new mini-series from Modern Romance™

Available this month:

BOUGHT: DESTITUTE YET DEFIANT
by Sarah Morgan

As soon as the delicate fabric whispered over her skin she gave a low moan of appreciation. She didn't need a mirror to know that it was going to look good. This dress would look good on anyone.

Hoping she wasn't going to fall flat on her face, she strolled forward, imitating the swaying, confident walk of the models. 'This store is trying to fleece you,' she said lightly. 'There's nothing but expensive stuff back here.'

'That's good.' In the middle of reading an email, Silvio didn't even glance up, and Jessie felt a rush of anticlimax, thrown by the fact he hadn't even looked at her.

'Well, you at least ought to tell me if you think it's worth the money.'

His glance was so fleeting that she almost missed it. 'You look fine.'

That was it? *That was all he was going to say?* Curiously deflated by his indifferent response, Jessie was about to turn away when she noticed the tension in his shoulders. Puzzled, she glanced at his face.

Finally he looked at her.

Self-conscious under his penetrating dark gaze, Jessie shifted awkwardly. 'What? There's no mirror so I couldn't look at myself. Am I wearing it the wrong way round or something?'

It was a moment before he answered, and when he did his voice was terse. 'There's nothing wrong with it. And this is going to take all day if we spend this long on each outfit.' He returned his attention to his phone and Jessie felt a rush of humiliation, all too aware that he'd paid the model more attention than he'd paid her.

BOUGHT: DESTITUTE YET DEFIANT

BY
SARAH MORGAN

All the characters in this book have no existence outside the imagination of the author, and have no relation whatsoever to anyone bearing the same name or names. They are not even distantly inspired by any individual known or unknown to the author, and all the incidents are pure invention.

First published in Great Britain 2010
Harlequin Mills & Boon Limited,
Eton House, 18-24 Paradise Road, Richmond, Surrey TW9 1SR

© Sarah Morgan 2010

ISBN: 978 0 263 87777 9

Harlequin Mills & Boon policy is to use papers that are natural, renewable and recyclable products and made from wood grown in sustainable forests. The logging and manufacturing process conform to the legal environmental regulations of the country of origin.

Printed and bound in Spain
by Litografia Rosés, S.A., Barcelona

BOUGHT: DESTITUTE YET DEFIANT

Sarah Morgan trained as a nurse, and has since worked in a variety of health-related jobs. Married to a gorgeous businessman, who still makes her knees knock, she spends most of her time trying to keep up with their two little boys but manages to sneak off occasionally to indulge her passion for writing romance. Sarah loves outdoor life and is an enthusiastic skier and walker. Whatever she is doing, her head is always full of new characters and she is addicted to happy endings.

Sarah also writes for Medical™ Romance

CHAPTER ONE

THEY'D come to kill her.

Two years of working on the seedier side of the city had honed her senses and taught her to keep herself sharp. She watched and she noticed—and she'd noticed them. A small group of men drinking too much, although she knew that would please Joe, who always hiked his prices when the punters were too drunk to notice. From her vantage point on the stage, she'd seen the notes changing hands, the bottles of whisky, the empty glasses and the glazed eyes but she'd just kept on singing, her voice pouring honey and whipped cream over anyone who bothered to listen. Ignoring the sick feeling in her gut that warned her that her time had finally run out, she sang about love and loss, knowing that the lonely men who frequented Joe's Bar knew far more about the second than the first.

And so did she.

It was an existence far from anyone's dreams but Jessie had stopped dreaming when she had been five years old.

'Hey, doll!' A man seated near the stage leered at her and waved a note. 'I fancy a private performance. Come over here and sing that song on my lap.'

Without missing a beat, Jessica backed away from him, flung her head back and belted out the final verse of the song with her eyes closed. As long as she had her eyes shut tight she could pretend that she was somewhere else. She wasn't singing to a crowd of leering men who had given up on life, she was singing to a packed stadium or opera house—to people who had paid the equivalent of a month's rent just to hear her voice. In that same fantasy she didn't have gnawing hunger pains in her stomach and she hadn't mended her cheap gold dress a hundred times. But most of all, she wasn't alone.

Someone out there was waiting for her.

Someone was going to pick her up from work and take her home somewhere warm, cosy and safe.

The song ended. She opened her eyes. And saw that someone *was* waiting for her.

Several men, but they weren't from her dreams—they were from a dark, terrifying nightmare.

And she knew that they'd come for her. Fear had shadowed her every step for so long that she felt worn out with anxiety—tired of looking over her shoulder.

The last warning she'd received had been a physical one, leaving her with bruises that had kept her home for a week.

But this time they weren't here to deliver a warning.

Feeling her mouth dry and her heart pound, Jessie reminded herself that she had a plan.

And a knife tucked in her suspender belt.

He sat in the back of the room, the darkness allowing him a rare moment of anonymity in a life lived in the spotlight. The previous night he'd walked the red carpet with a starlet on his arm. His business had made him a billionaire before he was thirty and he enjoyed the privileged existence of the super-rich, but his life had once been lived in places like this—surrounded by drunks, violence and the ever present threat of mortal danger. He'd grown up here—almost been sucked under by the greasy underbelly of society until he'd finally dragged himself, by sheer grit and determination, into a different world.

Another man might have chosen to lose those years, but he hated pretence of any sort and he carried the damage without apology, amused that the visible scars had proved as attractive to women as his dark, murky past.

Nothing aroused a woman's interest more than a bad boy, Silvio mused, knowing that if they'd been able to see inside his soul they would have run a mile. He was well aware that the women he mixed with liked the idea of danger, but not the reality. He also knew that the girl on the stage lived danger with every step and every breath.

He couldn't believe how far she'd sunk and he identified an emotion alien to him—guilt.

It was because of him that she was living this life.

His tension mounted as she moved in time to the beat, the subtle slide of her hips causing the man closest to him to lose his grip on his drink. The shatter of glass on the floor was a familiar sound and barely drew a glance from those around. Or maybe they were too numbed by the anaesthetising effects of alcohol to react.

Silvio sat in perfect stillness and the whisky on the table in front of him remained untouched. The glass was no more than a prop. Knowing what was to come, he couldn't afford to dull his senses. He also knew that whatever you escaped from today would still be waiting for you tomorrow, and he wasn't in need of a pause button.

He was a man who faced his mistakes, and he was facing one now.

He never should have left her.

No matter how difficult things had become between them,

no matter how deep her hatred of him, he should not have walked away.

The girl moved gracefully across the stage, seducing the audience, raising pulse rates and hopes in equal measure, her melting dark eyes and glossy mouth promising everything.

He'd watched her grow up. Seen her evolve from child to woman and nature hadn't just been generous in bestowing her gifts; she'd been lavish.

And Jessie exploited those gifts as she sang with passion and feeling, her incredible voice sending a tingle down the length of Silvio's spine. Watching her sway, he felt himself grow hard and the power of his response angered him because he'd never allowed himself to think of her like that.

He set his jaw, reminding himself that the chemistry they shared was a forbidden thing. Something neither of them had ever pursued and never would.

She was singing a ballad now, a slow, sultry rebuke to some man who had broken her heart, and he narrowed his eyes, knowing that she wasn't singing from experience. Jessie had never allowed a man anywhere near her heart.

She'd shut herself away emotionally when she had been a child. Only her brother had been able to penetrate the defensive shield she put between herself and the world.

Changing his mind about the neutralising effects of alcohol, Silvio reached for his glass. He downed it in one mouthful, his gaze never shifting from the girl on the stage.

Her ebony curls tumbled over her bare shoulders, the tantalising curves of her gorgeous body enhanced by a gold mini-dress that skimmed across the top of her incredible legs, leaving virtually nothing to the imagination.

Which was presumably intentional.

If a man had been searching for gold and discovered Jessie, he would have died happy.

The whisky burned his throat. Or was it the anger? Was this really what she'd done with her life in his absence? It took extraordinary will power to prevent himself from dragging her off the stage and hauling her out of there, away from the greedy eyes and lecherous minds.

But he didn't want to draw attention to himself. This was the last time, he promised himself. The last time she was standing on that stage.

The barman approached, but Silvio refused the offer of another drink with a faint shake of his head, his ice-cold gaze shifting from the girl to the group of men hovering around the table near him.

He knew every one of them, and he knew the danger she was facing.

He'd made a mistake, he thought grimly, thinking she'd be better off without him. When she'd ordered him out of her life, he should have ignored her. But it had been impossible to defend himself from her accusations because everything she'd said to him was true.

Silvio's mouth tightened, aware that he'd chosen the worst possible night to re-enter her life. Tonight was the third anniversary of her brother's death.

And he was responsible for that death.

Knowing she had no time, Jessica didn't waste any of it changing. Less than a minute after she'd slipped into the tiny cupboard that Joe laughingly called a dressing room, she was out of the door again, a thin cardigan covering the gold dress, trainers on her feet instead of heels. Her feet were crying from the vicious bite of the cheap shoes but she'd taught herself to ignore the pain. Her feet always hurt. Everything hurt. Tonight was no different.

Her heart was thundering, her palms were sweating but

she forced herself to focus, knowing that if she let the fear swallow her now, it would all be over.

And she owed this to Johnny.

Did they know what tonight was or was it a coincidence?

A lump formed in her throat as she thought of her brother. He'd always been there for her, but when he'd been in trouble she hadn't been able to save him—

Nursing her anger, she stepped out into the dark alleyway that ran along the back of the club, wondering whether this was going to be it for her. Was it going to end here in this grimy dark street amongst people who didn't care if she lived or died?

'Well, if it isn't our baby doll.' A slow male drawl came from the darkness and they emerged in a group, hoods over their heads, their faces obscured by the darkness. 'Do you have the money or are you ready to give us a private performance?'

Almost melting into the gutter with fear, Jessie managed to curve her lips into a smile. 'I don't have the money, but I have something else. Something better,' she said huskily, her voice smooth and full of promise. 'But you're not going to be able to claim it from there.' She gave the leader a provocative smile and beckoned him over. 'You'll need to come closer. One at a time.'

The man gave a short laugh. 'I knew you'd see sense. Why are you covering up that gold dress?' He sauntered towards her and Jessie forced herself to stand still and swallow the scream that was sitting at the base of her throat.

'It's raining.' She undid her cardigan and watched with satisfaction as his eyes popped out of his head and his brain stopped working. *Men were so predictable.* 'I'm cold.'

'You're not going to be cold for long, baby doll. There are six of us here to warm you up.' He stopped in front of her, all arrogant swagger, showing off in front of the other members of his gang. 'Where are the sexy heels?' He grabbed the cardigan and dragged it off her, the movement tearing the flimsy fabric. 'I really hope you haven't forgotten the sexy heels, babe, or I'm going to have to punish you.'

'I haven't forgotten the shoes,' Jessie said sweetly. 'In fact, I have them right here.' Really angry now because he'd ruined her only cardigan, she brought her hand round in front of her and jabbed the stiletto heel of her shoe hard into his groin.

With a howl of pain the man doubled up and then crumpled to the ground.

Jessica stood for a moment, slightly shocked by the sight of his writhing, agonised body. And then the shoe fell from her nerveless fingers and she ran.

Her trainers splashed through the puddles, the breath tore in her lungs and her knees were shaking so badly her legs wouldn't work properly.

From behind her came shouts, swearing, and then the thunder of feet as the rest of the men started in pursuit.

It was like being chased by a pack of wild hunting dogs, the terrifying inevitability of the ending slowing her pace.

Was it better to run and be caught from behind? Or better to turn and face the enemy?

She wanted to see what was happening—she didn't want to be blinded.

And then she slammed into something solid and a pair of strong hands caught her and stopped her flight.

Oh, God, somehow one of them had got around her. She was trapped.

It was all over.

For a single moment she froze, like a frightened bird caught in the talons of a hawk, and then the sound of shouts and running feet grew louder and she knew she had only moments.

Survival instincts took over.

Jessie lifted her knee to deliver a blow to his manhood but this man was quicker than her, anticipating the movement with a swift shift of his body. Without uttering a sound, he slid a strong arm around her waist and yanked her against him, ensuring that she had no room for manoeuvre.

Pressed against rock-hard muscle and powerful thighs, Jessie searched desperately for weakness and found none. At least, not in him. But being held against that powerful male body triggered an altogether different reaction inside her. Panic, yes. And something more intimate and twice as frightening. As her pelvis burned and melted Jessie struggled against his grip, shocked and appalled by the sudden flare of sexual awareness that gripped her. It must be something to do with adrenaline, she thought wildly. Something about the final moments before death making your senses more acute. Death was thundering down on her and she was aroused.

She was still trying to find an explanation for her inexplicable response when she became aware of the sudden change in the hard male body pressed against her.

So it was the same for him, she thought with a bitter smile. He did have a weakness after all—the same one all men had.

Turning that to her advantage, Jessie slid her hand down his powerful body and covered him with the flat of her hand.

His shock was only marginally greater than hers, and she heard the breath hiss through his teeth a fraction of a second before he slackened his hold. It was all she needed. Her fist landed against the side of his face and she was running again.

She took fewer than three steps before the arms closed over her again and he hauled her back like a rag doll.

'*Maledezione*, don't ever pull a stunt like that again!' The cold, furious voice penetrated her terror and Jessie felt a flicker of fear far, far deeper than anything she'd experienced before because she finally recognised who it was who held her.

Stunned, she stared into the face she'd just punched. 'Silvio—?'

'*Stai zitto!* Be quiet! Don't say a word,' he commanded, his fingers tightening on her wrists as the men finally caught up with them.

Jessie's mind went blank with shock.

Silvio Brianza.

Images exploded in her head. Images of the last time she'd seen him. Images she'd banished from her brain.

'Hey—thanks for catching her.' This was a different man from the one she'd injured with her shoe and Jessie wondered numbly whether his friend was still lying in the alley, clutching himself.

She didn't even care.

She was no longer worried about them.

The air was suddenly choked with an entirely different sort of tension and her emotions were focused on the man whose powerful body was pressed against every contour of hers.

Jessie tested his hold but it was like being held in a vice and her attempt to free herself drew a hiss of anger from him. She wished it had been anyone but Silvio who had come to her rescue.

'Let me go. I don't want your help.'

'Of course you don't—you're doing fine by yourself.' His scathing tone brought the colour rushing to her cheeks and Jessie felt a flash of humiliation that he should find her in this state.

'I can handle it,' she muttered, but she knew there was no

chance he was going to let her go. Silvio Brianza was too much a man to let a woman fight for him.

Thinking about him as a man was a mistake and the colour bloomed in her cheeks as she remembered how he'd felt against her hand.

Grateful for the darkness, Jessie gave a hysterical laugh.

She was about to be killed and she was thinking about sex again. Only this man could have that effect on her. He'd always made her think things she wasn't supposed to be thinking.

'You're going to be killed, Silvio.'

'I thought that was what you wanted.'

His reference to the last time they'd met made her shiver.

How many lonely nights had she spent planning his fate when the rest of the world had been sleeping? *A thousand ways to kill Silvio Brianza.*

Was that what she wanted? She couldn't think straight with the dangerous thrill of awareness gripping her shivering body.

All she knew was that the terrible fear had gone. Locked against his muscular frame, she felt safe. Which was ridiculous. She'd never been less safe in her life.

'Back off. She's ours.' The rough voice was thick with menace. 'You can hand her over and get back in your fancy car. We've got no quarrel with you.'

Fancy car?

Jessie turned her head, saw the low, sleek Ferrari parked at the end of the seedy alleyway. It was like a portal to another life. A reminder of how far Silvio had come.

He'd left all this behind. This wasn't his world any more. So what was he doing here?

Why had he picked tonight to step back into his past?

The man she'd stabbed with her shoe finally joined the rest

of his friends, his eyes burning with anger and resentment as he focused on Jessie.

She looked into those dull, drug glazed eyes and saw her own death.

Her thoughts were oddly detached as she prepared herself for the end. With Silvio by her side, there would be a fight, she knew that. But it was a fight they couldn't possibly win.

Would the end be quick?

Would it be a knife? A gun?

Suddenly she realised that she didn't want Silvio to die. Not for her.

She drew breath to speak but before she could utter a sound Silvio brought his mouth down on hers in a brief, scorching kiss.

Jessie was too shocked to protest, or perhaps her lack of resistance had something to do with the fact that her thoughts had skimmed perilously close to this exact scenario in the last few moments. Her lips parted beneath the pressure of his, hot, liquid pleasure diluting the fear. Far from resisting, she kissed him back passionately, her desperation as powerful as his, her demands every bit as urgent.

For most of her adolescence she'd fantasised about this. Even after that terrible night, when her world had darkened and her attitude towards him had irrevocably altered, perversely she'd still thought about it.

But of all the dreams she'd had, none of them had come close to the reality.

His mouth drove every thought from her head except one...

That if she had to choose a moment to die, this would be it.

Through a haze of desire she heard a snigger from the watching men. 'Now, that's just greedy,' one of them complained.

Her head still spinning from the kiss, Jessie didn't even realise Silvio had released her until he stepped forward out of the shadows. There was an air of menace attached to that simple, understated movement and she shivered as she watched, frightened and fascinated at the same time. He didn't speak or bluster—instead, he was terrifyingly cold, his spectacularly handsome face displaying not a single flicker of emotion as he confronted the men. And that, Jessie thought numbly, said everything there was to be said about Silvio Brianza. A lone warrior.

Her legs were threatening to give way, although whether it was from desire or fear she was no longer sure. All she knew was that she wanted to shout a warning. She wanted to warn him not to die for her, but her lips had been paralysed by the touch of his mouth and she couldn't think of anything except how it had felt to be kissed by him.

And then she realised that this scenario wasn't playing out the way she'd anticipated. Instead of attacking Silvio, the group was falling back. They'd lost the fierce bravado of a pack intent on a kill and instead they were just staring at him.

Water dripped from the gutter down the back of her neck and Jessie shivered as she tried to work out what was happening.

Why would six men retreat from one?

Confused, she glanced at Silvio and realised that he was standing in the faint shaft of light created by the final flickers of an exposed bulb presumably intended to provide light to the dank corners of the filthy alleyway.

And suddenly she realised what they'd seen. The distinctive scar that ran down one cheek—the only blemish in a face so insanely perfect that if it hadn't been for that one single flaw, his features could have been the work of Michelangelo.

Jessie strained her ears to hear what was being said but

the relentless drip of water from the surrounding roofs all but drowned out the words he was speaking and the eerie darkness made it impossible to read his lips.

At one point Jessie thought she heard someone mutter something that sounded like 'The Sicilian', but she couldn't be sure and they obviously had no interest in including her in the conversation.

Just when she was wondering whether she could slip away unnoticed, they all turned to look at her.

Jessie stood welded to the spot and for one crazy moment she wondered whether Silvio was going to join them. Strip away the expensive clothes and he had the credentials. He'd lived his early life among people like these. He'd led the most feared gang of all.

Those dangerous dark eyes fixed on her and for a fraction of a second he was a stranger to her. She saw what the others had seen. And what she saw was frightening.

Jessie sucked in a breath, reminding herself that, whatever their differences, this man would never hurt her physically.

Emotionally? Emotionally he'd achieved what a childhood lived rough hadn't managed to accomplish.

He'd broken her into tiny pieces.

Her eyes slid to the scar, her breathing stopped and they stared at each other. The tension in the air shifted and morphed into something different, something a thousand times more dangerous.

Without breaking eye contact, Silvio strolled towards her.

He was frighteningly calm and Jessie wanted to warn him not to turn his back on the men, but she didn't dare snap the tension that held them all immobile.

As he reached her he lifted a hand and stroked her hair away from her face, the gesture oddly out of place in such a tense situation. His touch was both deliberate and possessive, as if he was making a statement about their relationship, and she didn't understand that because they didn't have a relationship any more.

It had been smashed in that grimy room exactly three years earlier, over her brother's lifeless body.

Then his hand dropped. '*Andiamo.* Let's go. Get in the car,' he commanded, and Jessie obeyed, not because she wanted to get in the car, but because she was as mesmerised by his aura of authority as the gang members. He dominated this godless, lawless environment with the sheer force of his presence and Jessie slid into the sumptuous warmth of the Ferrari, feeling as though she were stepping into another world. Moments later he joined her and she wasn't sure whether the deep growl came from the engine or the depths of his throat. All she knew was that she'd been wrong about his mood.

He wasn't calm.

He wasn't calm at all.

Forced into close proximity by the confines of the car she could tell that he was struggling with a raging anger and that knowledge unsettled her because in all the years she'd known him, she'd never seen him like this. Never seen that icy control slide. Not once. Not even that night when their relationship had hit rock bottom.

'Silvio—'

'Don't say a word.' He cut her off before she could even begin her sentence, his voice strangely thickened, his knuckles white on the wheel. He didn't glance in her direction. Instead he kept his eyes fixed on the road, speeding through the back streets of London as if he were competing for a Formula 1 title.

Jessie was tempted to point out that there wasn't a lot of

point in rescuing her from one threat only to kill them both in a car wreck, but she kept her mouth shut.

Why him?

Why did it have to be him who had rescued her?

Now that the immediate danger had passed, her thoughts were impossibly confused. The adrenaline rushing around her body had been diluted by another hormone and the only thing in her head was that kiss. Her body was still trembling from the pressure of his mouth against hers and the more she remembered of her wild, crazy response, the more appalled she was. Had he noticed her reaction? She shrank in her seat, hoping that he'd been too distracted to register just how enthusiastically she'd played her part.

Disgust slithered over her bones and settled in the core of her like a cold, hard stone.

Had she no shame?

How was it possible to respond like that to someone you'd spent three years hating? Her brain was like a slide show— one minute she was remembering the breath-stealing moment when his dark head had lowered to hers, the next she was seeing her brother's face.

Shocked, confused and ripped apart with self-loathing, Jessie realised that the one thing she wasn't thinking of was the six men who had just tried to kill her.

And that didn't make sense, did it?

Her gaze slid to Silvio.

He was just one man.

Why did she feel safe?

She swallowed a hysterical laugh, wondering why she needed to ask herself that question.

The visible markers of success hadn't changed who he was. The expensive watch on his wrist, the car he was driving—none of those things had shaped the man. Underneath the exterior of smooth sophistication that enabled him to blend with the upper echelons of society, Silvio was solid steel. Hard, tough and the very essence of what it meant to be a man.

She felt safe because she *was* safe. Physically. Any woman would be safe with him, although perhaps only she really understood who he really was.

Just looking at him made her feel guilty and Jessie tore her eyes away from him and looked behind her. Not that she thought for one moment anyone would be following the Ferrari. It would be like sending a donkey in pursuit of a race-horse.

'They called you "the Sicilian".' Unable to help herself, she cast another look at his profile. Looking at him was an irresistible compulsion. 'It's so long since you had anything to do with that life but your reputation still frightens them. They knew you.' She stared in fascination, wondering why she wasn't more afraid of him herself.

Was it because she couldn't see the scar?

From this angle the damaged skin was invisible, his features almost impossibly perfect.

Perfect, but cold.

Up until tonight she would have said he didn't feel—but it was evident that he was feeling something.

Jessie wondered why he was so angry. 'Why did you come here tonight?'

'I heard a rumour about a pack of trouble and a girl with a golden voice.' He shifted gears viciously, coaxed the car round a tight corner and accelerated away so fast that Jessie's head thumped gently against the head rest.

'I wasn't looking for trouble.'

His eyes were fixed straight ahead of him. 'How much did he owe them?'

Jessie gave a twisted smile, not at all surprised that he knew the truth.

She didn't waste time pretending he'd misunderstood. Neither did she ask him how he knew. He knew everything. This man had contacts at every strata of society—a network that would have made both social climbers and the police force weep with envy.

'Forty thousand,' she said flatly, wishing the sum didn't sound so terrifying. 'It was twice that, but I've paid back half. I'm late with a payment. That's why they came after me tonight.' She gave him no details. Didn't elaborate. But he knew. He was a man who'd known hunger, violence and deprivation and, in the fleeting second before he controlled his reaction, she saw the murderous flash of anger in his eyes.

'You paid them?' The question hissed through his lips and Jessie was reminded that this man was twice as danger-ous as the men he'd rescued her from.

'I didn't exactly have a choice.'

He changed gears with a savage movement of his hand. 'But you could have gone to the police.'

The dark streets flashed past and Jessie wondered if he even realised he'd just driven straight through a red light. 'That would have made things worse.'

'For whom? Law-abiding citizens shouldn't be afraid of the police, Jessie. Or were you afraid you'd be arrested?' The contempt in his tone baffled her until she saw his gaze flick briefly to her exposed thighs—saw the raw fury—and sud-denly understood his meaning.

He thought she—

That was why he was so angry?

Jessie was so shocked that for a moment she couldn't respond. 'What sort of job do you think I'm doing?'

'Presumably the same job as the rest of the girls in that club.'

He thought she was a prostitute.

She leaned her head back against the seat and started to laugh. It was that or cry and there was no way she was ever crying in front of this man. All her tears had been shed in private.

'You think it's funny?' His tone savage, he drove the car harder still and Jessie wondered why it bothered her so much that he thought that of her.

'I use what God gave me. What's wrong with that?' It was a stupid thing to say. Flippant, provocative—like dangling a piece of raw meat in front of a hungry wolf—and the moment the words left her mouth she wanted to suck them back in. But it was too late for that. Too late to wish that everything was different between them.

Too late to wish that the past hadn't happened.

And perhaps it was safer this way. If his opinion of her was rock bottom then it would protect them both from the dangerous chemistry that had flickered round the edges of their relationship like a force field.

She didn't want that.

He didn't want that.

He brought the car to an abrupt halt and when he looked at her the red blaze of fury in his eyes made her shrink against the seat in instinctive retreat.

'If you were that desperate for money,' he said thickly, 'you could have come to me. It didn't matter what happened between us. None of that mattered. If you were in trouble, you should have contacted me.'

'You are the last person on this earth I would ever ask for help.' But the words came out as a whisper because she was too overwhelmed by her feelings to manage anything stronger or more convincing.

Self-loathing mingled with a desperate yearning that frightened her.

She didn't want to feel like this.

'Pride can kill, Jessie.'

'It isn't about pride! Even if I'd wanted to contact you, I wouldn't have known how. I don't know you any more.' Neither did she know herself. 'You're always surrounded by clever people and security staff. Although why you need the security staff, I don't understand.' She turned to look at him and then immediately looked away because one glance at his mouth made her think of that kiss. 'Why do you employ security staff? You don't exactly need help, do you? Or are you worried about dirtying your expensive suit?'

'Don't change the subject,' he said harshly. 'Were you really prepared to die rather than contact me? Is that the honest truth?'

Jessie stared in front of her, realising with a flash of surprise that they were parked on the pavement near her block of flats. 'You know why I didn't contact you.'

'*Sì*, I know. You hate me.' His tone was flat but his grip on the wheel didn't relax. 'You blame me for everything.'

'Not everything—just that one thing. Do you know what tonight is?' Her voice shook with emotion and his eyes flashed.

'Do you think I'd forget this date? Does it help you to know I blame myself every bit as much as you do?' The rain pelted onto the car, blurring their surroundings.

Like tears, Jessie thought as she stared at the water pouring over the windscreen. 'No. It doesn't help.' Nothing helped.

The memory of that night hovered between them like a menacing storm cloud waiting to unleash something terrible and Jessie unclipped her seat belt and opened the car door, on the run from memories and a conversation she didn't want to have.

'Thanks for the lift.' She didn't say 'home' because she didn't think of this place as home. It was just the place she slept—for now. Until she moved on—which she did regularly.

It was raining hard now, the litter-strewn pavements slick with it, the graffiti on the walls glistening under a glowing orange streetlamp.

Jessie felt ridiculous standing there, soaked to the skin in her cheap gold dress. Next to the sleek Ferrari and the equally sleek billionaire she felt appallingly self-conscious.

Jessie the prostitute.

Was that really how she looked?

So much for her fantasy about singing to packed stadiums or opera houses.

She was as far removed from that as the average woman singing into her hairbrush. As far removed from that as she was from the man who was now striding round the car to her.

His eyes glittered in the ominous light. Ignoring the rain, Silvio removed his coat and slung it around her shoulders. Pulling it closed, he covered her up, every millimetre of her—as if he couldn't bear to look. 'You do realise that this is the last place in the world that any sane woman would choose to come to alone at night?'

The coat overwhelmed her, falling almost to the ground and covering her hands. 'They tracked me down. I had to move. They don't know I live here.' She rolled the sleeves back methodically, trying to find her hands—and then she froze, the truth slamming into her.

He knew she lived here.

Jessie felt her face drain of colour and met his diamond-hard eyes with dawning horror. 'You didn't ask for directions.' Her voice was a cracked whisper. 'How did you know where to drop me?'

'I make it my business to know things,' he said grimly. 'And if I know, you can be sure that those animals know too. I calculate we probably have less than ten minutes to clear out your things before they get here. Move!'

CHAPTER TWO

THE ground floor.

She was living on the ground floor.

Silvio stood in perfect stillness as she undid the bolts on the door, struggling with anger almost too big to contain. He knew that his ability to control his emotions was one of the things that separated him from those animals they'd left behind, and yet right now he didn't feel so different from those men. What had she said to him?

I use what God gave me.

Remembering the careless way she'd thrown those words at him, Silvio turned away from her, not trusting himself to speak or even look at her. In his head he was seeing Jessie the child, clinging to her brother and not understanding where her comfortable, familiar life had gone. He couldn't reconcile that vision of vulnerable innocence with reality—he kept seeing Jessie in the tight gold dress, using what God gave her.

The innocence had gone.

He'd known from the moment he'd taken her mouth and felt her wild, uninhibited response.

Just thinking about it had an immediate impact on his body and Silvio swore in Italian, exasperated by his inability to switch off that part of himself. Knowing that his priority had to be to get her away from here, he inhaled deeply and forced himself to focus on what was important.

Saving her life.

Turning back to her, he saw that she was shivering under his coat, but he knew there was little he could do about that. Even though she sold her favours to men, he knew instinctively that if he touched her now he'd risk adding another bruise to the one already developing on the right side of his face.

It had come as no surprise that she knew how to punch.

He'd taught her.

She undid the last bolt and pushed open the door. 'There. Home, sweet home. You can go now. Thanks for the ride.'

'I'm not going anywhere.' They were a sitting target in the dimly lit walkway and he wasn't leaving her there.

Silvio glanced back at the gleaming paint of his black Ferrari, the car as visible and out of place as an alien spaceship in a children's playground.

'If you're worried about your toy, Silvio, just go and play with it,' she said tartly, gasping as he yanked her back and stepped in front of her. 'What are you doing? I'm not inviting you in for coffee if that's what you're hoping. You had one kiss for free. That's all you're getting.' The bravado hid an ocean of fear and Silvio wondered how long it would take her to admit that she was scared.

'That kiss saved your life.' Even it had been at the expense of his own mental stability.

Taking what he assumed to be a last look at his car, Silvio went into the flat first, knowing exactly what he would find.

Much of his childhood had been spent in places exactly like this—bars at the window, locks on the door and a board hammered over the letter box because whatever anyone wanted to post through your door, it sure as hell wasn't going to be a letter.

Being back here was harder than he was prepared to admit, even to himself.

It was dank and small and it took him less than five seconds to reassure himself that no one was inside.

Closing the blinds and securing the front door, he turned with a growl. 'You shouldn't be living on the ground floor.' The moment the words left his mouth he could have bitten his tongue because he of all people should have known why she'd chosen this position.

He pressed his fingers to his temples, tasting regret. Sensitive words didn't come easily to him but he was fairly sure he could have done better than that if he hadn't been distracted.

Anticipating her reaction, he cast her a look and she looked straight back at him, her eyes dark pools of defiance.

'What? If you're waiting for me to crumble, Silvio, you're going to be waiting a long time. I'm tough as nails.'

Silvio shook his head in disbelief, not knowing whether to laugh or strangle her. 'There isn't time for you to crumble,' he said evenly. 'You've got five minutes to pack anything that's important to you. Then we're leaving.' A flash of gold dress and creamy skin knocked the words out of his brain and he looked away quickly. The fact that he needed to do so told him just how close to the edge he was.

On reflection, he wished he'd found another way to secure her safety other than by kissing her.

Never before in his life had he had such a slippery grip on control and he knew that if he saw her in that outrageously sexy dress he'd start thinking of all those men looking at her...

How many of them had had their hands on her?

And why had he waited three years to come looking for her? Why had he thought she'd be better without him in her life?

Apparently unaware of his torment, she reached into a cupboard. The coat slipped from her shoulders and the movement of her body gave him a flash of suspender belt. And something else.

With a soft curse Silvio stepped forward and stuck his hand up her dress, ignoring her outraged gasp. He stepped back with the knife in his hand, his mood so dangerous that he didn't trust himself to be close to her.

'*Maledezione*, what is this?'

'It's a knife.' Her gaze challenged him. 'You should know—it isn't as if you haven't seen one before.'

'You shouldn't be carrying this.' His fingers toyed with the blade, the glint of metal winking at him mockingly. 'If I hadn't turned up when I did…'

'I would have used it if I had to.'

Thinking about what would have happened if she'd produced a knife sent ice through his veins.

He'd almost lost her.

A chorus of vicious barking from outside the flat reminded him that they had no time for reflection or recrimination and Silvio slipped the knife into his pocket and retrieved his coat from the floor.

'Find yourself a coat that fits. I assume you have one. And hurry up.' He wondered whether he'd been foolish to allow her to come here, but then he reminded himself that they needed her passport.

'I don't understand the hurry. It's going to take me more than five minutes to find somewhere new to live. This is premium property, Silvio—not easy to come by.' Pulling open a cupboard, she removed a mug and waved it at him.

'Water? I can't offer you coffee—they turned the gas and electric off last week.'

'You've just lost thirty seconds of packing time,' Silvio ground out, prowling to the window and staring into the badly lit concrete walkway that led to the flats. The area made him shiver.

How many times had she risked her life crossing that litter-strewn concrete desert late at night?

'I take it that's a no.' With a careless shrug, she put the mug down on a small table and Silvio glanced back at her, frowning as he saw the red bruising on her knuckles.

'I'd forgotten about your hand.'

'My hand is fine. How's your face?'

'My face is fine.' Struggling with emotions he didn't know he was capable of feeling, Silvio crossed to the small fridge and yanked it open, glaring with disbelief at the empty shelves. 'What do you eat?'

'I usually eat out,' Jessie said blithely, her slender frame telling a different story. 'I can't get through the week without dining in at least one Michelin-starred restaurant.'

Ignoring her sarcasm, Silvio reminded himself that his priority was getting her out of this place, not sorting out deficiencies in her diet. 'Where's the freezer compartment?'

'No freezer compartment. You'll just have to take your gin and tonic without the ice. Sorry for any inconvenience.'

If the situation hadn't been so urgent he would have admired her courage.

Or maybe it was just that she didn't know how much danger she was in.

And then she switched on another light and he saw the dark shadows under her eyes.

She knew.

The fact that she was frightened dug deep into his gut. Her

life choices were coming back to haunt her and regret sliced through him because if he'd been here, everything would have been different.

He'd thought that leaving was the best thing he could do for her. Now he saw it had been the worst.

'That's another minute wasted,' he drawled softly. 'Never mind—the ice will have to wait until we're at my place.' The bruising on her hand would be worse but he'd have to find some other way of dealing with it. It was better than this nervous tension.

'I'm not going with you, Silvio.' She turned on the tap, filled the mug full of water and drank thirstily. But the hand holding the mug was shaking. 'Get out of my life.'

'I did that once before. It didn't work out so well, did it?'

'It worked perfectly for me.'

'I'm back in your life, Jessie, whether you like it or not.'

'You can't afford me, Silvio. You might be rich but I'm out of your league.' Her allusion to her dubious lifestyle stoked his anger. He wanted to push her up against the wall and demand to know why she'd allowed this to happen. He wanted to know why it had all gone so wrong. But he knew the answer to that one.

He was responsible. Because of him, she'd given up caring. Because he'd allowed her to send him away, he hadn't been able to protect her.

Guilt crashed down on him and he heaved it away, knowing it to be a poor friend—a stifling, useless weight that achieved nothing. Keep moving forward—wasn't that how he'd lived his life?

'Another thirty seconds gone. I hope you travel light.' Silvio prowled back to the window and lifted the blinds just enough to give him visual access.

The first thing he noticed was that a small crowd had

gathered around his car. The second was that a battered black van with no lights had pulled up at the far end of the street.

He swore in Italian. 'You're out of time, Cinderella. Get your passport.'

'I've told you—I'm not going with you.'

'Now!' He thundered the word and saw her flinch. 'Before both our brains are splattered over your wall. Move!'

'I—'

'So help me, Jess, my reputation will only protect us for so long. After that we need something a little more concrete. If you say one more word I'll shoot you myself.' Distracted by the neckline of her gold dress, he was finding it hard to concentrate. 'Get your passport!'

'I don't have a passport! You're the one who joined the jet set, not me!' She yelled the words at him, her cheeks flushed and her eyes defiant. 'Why would I need a passport? International travel isn't exactly high on my list of priorities.'

Acutely conscious of the vulnerability revealed by that statement, Silvio hunted for a sensitive response but in the end resorted to practicality. 'I'll get you a passport.'

'I've told you, I'm not—'

'You come of your own free will or I carry you,' he growled thickly. 'Your choice.'

'You call that a choice?' A car door slammed and she jumped. Her eyes flew to his and he saw her terror.

'Discussion over.' He grabbed her wrist but she dug her heels in.

'Wait—there's something I need…' Wrenching her wrist out of his grip, she scrambled onto the rickety table and removed a shoebox from a cupboard.

Averting his eyes from another flash of stocking and smooth thigh, Silvio stared through the blinds and saw the van doors open. Six of them. The same six.

Pulling out his phone, he made a call, the exchange of words taking all of five seconds to complete.

Seeing Jessie teetering on the table, he reached out and swung her down. He tried to take the shoebox from her but she snarled at him like a lioness protecting a litter of cubs, clutching the box so tightly that her fingers were white and the lid of the box crumpled slightly.

'Whatever is in that box, it isn't worth risking your life for,' he thundered, but he let her keep the box. 'Does the bathroom window open? Is there a way out of the back?' He knew there would be, because there was no way Jessie would live anywhere that didn't have several exits.

'This way.' She vanished through a door and Silvio followed her, bumping his head on the doorframe and squashing inside the tiny bathroom he'd seen briefly when he'd checked for intruders. There was barely room for one of them, let alone two.

She wasn't coming back here, he promised himself savagely as she pushed up the window and dropped silently onto the grass, the movement affording him another glimpse of her gorgeous legs. He was going to make sure of it.

He followed her through the window, grabbed her hand and hauled her back towards the front of the building.

She dug her heels in. 'Not that way. They're waiting for us.'

'They've gone in the front.' Hearing the splintering of wood, Silvio scooped her up in his arms and carried her towards the car just as the sound of police sirens split the air. She was still clutching the shoebox and her hair brushed against his cheek, the scent sending a thousand forbidden memories skimming across his senses.

'What's in that damn box, Jess?'

'Stuff. Silvio, drop me and get out of here…' Her voice cracked and she struggled in his arms. 'You don't want to be involved in this. You don't need those headlines in your fancy new life. Leave me.'

It was his first glimpse of the real Jessie—kind, caring Jessie, the terrified, frightened girl he'd met when he'd still been a wild teenager making all the wrong choices. 'I'm not leaving you again, Jess. Get used to it. And with a background like mine it's a bit late to worry about what the media are going to write.' He unlocked the Ferrari with the press of a button and dropped her and her precious shoebox onto the passenger seat.

The movement was too much for the cheap gold dress and the seam split, testing his restraint by exposing a generous section of bare midriff and the shimmer of sexy underwear.

Deciding that he would rather have faced a gun, Silvio recoiled and slammed the door.

Without looking over his shoulder, he slid behind the wheel and accelerated away from his past, keeping his eyes fixed forward.

Something soft was pressed against her cheek and she felt deliciously warm. If this was heaven, it was a great place.

'Jess?' A rough male voice came from nearby. 'Jessie, can you hear me?'

Jessie assumed she was supposed to respond but she was just too warm and comfortable to move and anyway the voice sounded angry and she preferred to stay in the protective clouds of sleep where nothing could touch her.

'*Maledezione*, I should have removed that wet dress. She's been asleep for too long.'

'Could be shock, boss. And she's warm enough under the blanket.' Another voice, this one deferential. 'Do you want me to call the doc?'

'No, not yet.' The hard voice again. The angry one. Only

this time there was a hint of something else in those steely tones.

Worry?

Had she really slept that long?

Surely not. She never, ever slept.

She only ever dozed, kept awake by her tormented thoughts and the ever-present threat of danger.

Drifting in that blissful land between sleep and wakefulness, Jessie realised that she'd slept because she'd felt secure. For the first time in as long as she could remember, she knew she was safe.

Jessie opened her eyes and met his. Her heart emptied itself into that one, single look and she saw the answering flare of awareness in his eyes. There wasn't a sound in the room, nothing but the hammering of her heart and his sharp, indrawn breath.

And then she remembered.

She remembered why she couldn't feel this way.

He withdrew from her instantly, the hardening of his mouth the only indication that he'd read her thoughts.

'There's a bathroom through that door.' His tone was neutral and he gestured to an archway. 'Dressing room through there. Help yourself to anything that fits. When you've freshened up, we'll talk.'

'Dressing room?' Jessie sat up, realising that the warmth and comfort had been delivered by an opulent velvet throw in a rich shade of aubergine. Underneath she was still wearing the minuscule gold dress and next to her was the shoebox. With a rush of relief, she curled her fingers over it, pulling it closer.

Silvio watched her for a long, disturbing moment and then a man appeared in the doorway and he glanced towards him. 'Yes?'

'Chief Inspector Warren on the phone. Says it's urgent.'

'I'll call him back.' Silvio turned back to her and Jessie stared at him in disbelief.

'You were the one who called the police?'

'That's what they're there for, Jess. Dealing with crime. I need to return this call.' He glanced at his watch. 'If you need anything, shout. I'll be outside.'

'No, wait—we can't stay here. If they know where I live then they probably followed us here—they're dangerous…' Panic fluttered inside her like the wings of a trapped butterfly and his lips curved into a sardonic smile.

'I'm dangerous too,' he said softly. 'Or have you forgotten that?'

She'd forgotten nothing and her eyes lifted to his cold, handsome face and she shivered.

'You used the police as delaying tactics but that won't work for long. They want money from me—and they want…' She couldn't bring herself to articulate the rest of the sentence and she didn't need to because they both knew what she was referring to.

His eyes darkened and he turned abruptly and strode to the window, as if he were struggling with something. 'If you can't even say the word then perhaps you should consider changing your profession.'

She should have corrected him but she didn't want to.

Let him think it.

His revulsion and contempt would help create the distance she needed.

'What is this place, anyway?' She looked around the room, seeing space and luxury. 'Is it a hotel or something? Clever. They wouldn't look for me in a place as fancy as this.'

'It's my apartment.' He answered without turning. 'And you're lying in my bed.'

His apartment?

His bed?

Trying not to think about the bed part, Jessie swallowed, kicking herself mentally for being so stupid. For not knowing that apartments this big existed. Feeling gauche and unsophisticated, she shrugged carelessly. 'So—business must be good if you can afford a place like this.'

'Business is fine.'

Jessie pushed her hair out of her eyes, willing to bet he'd never had anyone like her in his fancy apartment before.

It was a supremely male domain. Nothing girly here. No pink or frills or concessions towards anything soft. It was upmarket and expensive, luxurious in every sense. And surprisingly minimalist. The corners of her mouth flickered. 'I didn't think you could live without your gadgets. Where's the flat-screen TV?'

'Hidden. Why?' Finally he turned, his handsome face devoid of expression, his dark eyes revealing nothing of his thoughts. 'Do you want to watch something?'

'No.' Her eyes were fixed on the modern fireplace that was a feature of the back wall. It wasn't lit, but the breath had become trapped in her throat and she stared for a moment, forcing herself to breathe calmly, knowing his eyes were on her. Watching. 'Stylish.' She forced the word between dry lips and he gave a brief nod, apparently satisfied by her response.

Shaken by how hard it was to hide her feelings from him, Jessica reminded herself that she needed to be careful.

He knew her too well. 'This is really your home?'

'One of them.'

Jessica tried to imagine owning more than one place like this and gave a twisted smile. She couldn't have felt more out of place if he'd dropped her into the jungle in her cheap gold dress. In fact, she probably would have felt safer in the jungle—she was used to living amongst wild animals. But this...she glanced around the acres of space...was an alien environment.

'You don't need to feel uncomfortable, Jess.'

'I don't feel uncomfortable.' The words were defiant and wasted because they both knew she was lying.

He sighed. 'And you don't need to be scared.'

'I'm not scared.'

She was terrified.

Not of the group of men that were so intent on spilling her blood, not even of this swanky apartment. What frightened her was him.

Her feelings.

They were too tangled, too complex, too dark...

It was a cruel twist of fate that had made him her rescuer.

Suddenly she knew she couldn't stay on this bed any longer—*his bed*—and she threw off the velvet cover and padded silently over to him, feeling his eyes follow her every move.

It shouldn't have bothered her.

Men did that.

They watched her.

She'd taught herself to handle it and it no longer worried her—sometimes it was even useful because it meant that her tips were bigger. This time it was different.

This man was different.

'Where are we?' She wasn't interested in where they were, but she looked out of the window because it gave her something to focus on other than the man.

It took her a moment to react because the view was so very different from what she'd been expecting. This was a rich man's view—London at its sparkling, night-time best, a vibrant city dressed like a woman ready for a glamorous date, all high heels and diamonds.

His world.

Far beneath her, the river Thames curled in a ribbon and Jessica gave a gasp and recoiled.

As if he'd been waiting for precisely this reaction he curled strong hands over her shoulders and steadied her. 'It's all right.'

Panic choked her and she gasped for breath, teetering on the precipitous edge between sanity and hysteria. 'It's not all right! It's not all right, Silvio! You brought me to the top floor!' Her voice rose and she snatched in several short breaths. 'How could you do that? How could you? I have to get out of here!' She tried to drag herself out of his arms but his fingers bit into her arms and he shook her slightly.

'Jess, listen to me.' His voice was commanding, his grip preventing her from running. She would have gone over the balcony if she'd had the chance and he knew it. 'You're not trapped. You're safe.'

There was roaring in her ears and she lifted her hand to her mouth, her breathing so rapid that the world started to spin.

She heard Silvio swear softly and then he hauled her across the room and yanked open a door. In front of her was a curving metal slide, like something from a child's playground. She stared at it blankly and she heard him sigh.

'If you sit on it, you'll be on the ground floor in less than four seconds. I designed it myself.' Still with his hand around her wrist he dragged her back to the glass wall overlooking the river, hit a button and the whole thing slid open.

The cold air and driving rain made her gasp but he pulled her onto the balcony and gestured. 'Staircase.' His tone was forceful, his gaze compelling as he tried to penetrate the terror that was eating her up. 'From this bedroom alone there are three exits. Do you understand me, Jess? Three exits.

There are another nine from the rest of the apartment. It isn't possible to be trapped in here.'

Another soaking of rain was turning the cheap gold dress into a sodden rag and she was shivering again, but Jessie managed a nod.

In terms of acknowledgement it wasn't much, but it was obviously enough for him because he drew her back inside, hit the button again and once again the outside world vanished and the glass wall closed her inside the cocoon of climate controlled luxury.

Humiliation swamped her. 'Sorry…'

'Jessie—you were dragged out of a burning house when you were five years old,' he said grimly. 'Don't apologise to me. I know why you sleep on the ground floor. I know why you don't like tall buildings, but you're safe here. I know it's not the ground floor, but you can't be trapped. Trust me.'

He was the last man in the world she wanted to trust, but what choice did she have? At this moment in time she was in too much of a mess to be fussy.

If she left his protection, she'd be dead.

Without releasing her hand, Silvio strode purposefully into the bathroom. He hit a button on the wall and hot, scented water swirled into the large tub.

Jessie wanted to say something but she had no idea what.

He stared at her frozen features with a mixture of concern and exasperation. 'You're cold. You're wet. You've had a long day. Get out of that damn dress, soak in the bath, close your eyes. Then you can eat. Judging from the contents of your fridge, you need it.' His eyes raked her face and then he cautiously released her wrist, still watching her. 'After that we'll talk.'

Jessie's teeth were chattering. 'What's the point in talking? You'll do what you want to do.'

A sardonic smile touched his beautiful mouth. 'Yes, you're right. I will. Get in the bath, Jess.'

Did she look that bad?

She scraped her soaking hair away from her face, knowing that she must look like a drowned rat. *Knowing that she owed him thanks.* Despite her gratitude for his intervention, she just couldn't say the words. Showing gratitude to a man she hated proved impossible. She was still trying to force the words past her uncooperative lips when he gestured to a heated cabinet by the bath.

'Towels. Anything else you need, shout.' He paused by the door—cool, sophisticated and very much at home in this world. 'Perhaps you'd better not lock the door.'

He closed the door behind him and Jessie immediately locked it.

Why had he suddenly reappeared in her life? And why was he helping her? After the things she'd said to him, she hadn't expected ever to see him again.

It couldn't be guilt or regret.

She knew that Silvio Brianza didn't have a conscience.

She leaned her forehead against the locked door, embarrassed by her loss of control and wishing it hadn't been him who had witnessed it. Then she laughed. No one but him would have understood. But Silvio had been there after the fire. He'd been living in the care home where she and her orphaned teenage brother had been taken after the tragedy that had shattered their young lives.

They'd lost everything, and everyone, and they'd been thrust into a world that had been both harsh and cruelly unfamiliar.

Jessie turned and looked at the bath, tempted by the froth of luxurious bubbles and the prospect of steaming water. How long had it been since she'd dipped herself in hot water?

Too long. And never in a bath like this one. To just lie in a bath and relax, knowing that someone else was watching for danger…

Despite the sleep she felt exhausted, but she knew she couldn't stay here. Not with him. It was out of the question. He was her enemy.

She rubbed her fingers over her lips, trying to erase the memory of that kiss—telling herself that she had no reason to feel guilty. *He'd* kissed *her*. Not the other way round.

But she hadn't fought him off, had she?

Confused and angry with herself, she stripped off the gold dress, ripping it further in the process. She was *not* going to feel guilty. It wasn't as if she'd gone to him for help. She hadn't. Even when she'd been at her lowest point, she hadn't allowed herself to approach him.

And she'd had no choice but to accept his help tonight. If she hadn't, she'd be lying bleeding in that alleyway.

Survival, she reminded herself grimly. That was what her life was about.

Survival.

Reasoning that she wasn't going to get far in a soaking-wet gold dress, Jessie stripped it off and slid into the bath, moaning with rapture as the hot water soothed and warmed her skin.

Just for a minute, she promised herself as she slid deeper under the foam. What harm could it do?

But she couldn't relax. She was too wound up after what had happened and luxuriating in warm bubbles was something she'd never done before. It felt…decadent. She shampooed her hair quickly and in less than two minutes she was out of the bath and drying herself in a soft warm towel. Eyeing the damp gold dress on the floor, she faced the fact that she was going to have to borrow something to wear.

Her instinct was to refuse his offer, but how could she?

What clothes she had were back in her grim little flat. And she wouldn't miss any of them.

Wondering why she was worrying about modesty when he thought she was a prostitute, Jessie wrapped herself in a long bathrobe before emerging cautiously from the bathroom.

Her precautions proved unnecessary because the bedroom was empty, the lighting dimmed to a warm, intimate glow.

She stared at the bed, her wayward mind conjuring up images she didn't want to see.

Was this where he brought his women?

Did he kiss them the way he'd kissed her?

Forcing aside that unsettling thought, she snatched up the shoebox she'd rescued from her flat and tucked it under her arm. Then she padded over to the dressing room, aware that the last place she'd lived would have fitted into this space with room to spare. It was huge.

A door had been left open for her and she peeped inside, like a nervous child exploring its mother's wardrobe, afraid of being caught.

Her mouth fell open because she'd never seen anything like it, even in her dreams.

There were racks of shoes stored in transparent boxes; jumpers and T-shirts in a rainbow of colours, all perfectly folded, and rails of shimmering, glamorous dresses.

Jessie reached out a hand and touched one of the dresses, the silk sliding over her fingers like fluid. There was nothing cheap here. Nothing suitable for the life she led.

The clothes went with the apartment and the apartment was the domain of the super-rich. She bent to tuck her battered, cardboard shoebox safely into the corner of the cupboard, out of sight.

'Are you all right?' His voice came from behind her and Jessie jumped as if she'd been caught stealing, clutching the edges of the dressing gown together at her throat to make sure that not a millimetre of flesh was exposed.

'I'm fine.'

'You were quick.'

She stiffened defensively, not wanting to admit that she was too jumpy to relax. 'I spent as long as I needed.'

'Why aren't you dressed?'

Jessie gave a humourless laugh and glanced over her shoulder at the rails of clothes. 'Because I couldn't see anything suitable.'

His gaze slid to the rails of clothes and a faint smile touched his mouth. 'That's a very female remark. A closet full of clothes and nothing to wear.'

'They're not right.'

'Nothing fits?'

'I have no idea if anything fits me! I haven't tried any of them on.'

'Why not?'

'Because I can't wear any of that stuff, Silvio!' Suddenly she wished she were wearing her heels. At least then she wouldn't have felt quite so small and insignificant next to him. Or maybe she would. Acknowledging that her feelings of inferiority came from the inside, Jessie glared at him, exasperated that he had so little clue as to how she was feeling. 'Where am I going to wear fancy stuff like this? I can hardly walk around the streets wearing a floor-length gown, can I?'

'You're not going to be walking around the streets.' Studying her face, he leaned against the doorframe, supremely relaxed and indecently good-looking.

Jessie noticed that he'd showered and changed, his dark hair slightly spiky from the water, his lean, powerful legs encased in clean, black jeans. An expensive watch glinted from beneath the cuff of his tailored shirt and Jessie wondered idly how much it had cost him.

More than she'd earned in her lifetime.

He looked as sleek and expensive as the apartment he lived in and the car he drove.

But most importantly of all, he was comfortable here. As comfortable as he'd been in the dirty alley. He was able to move between the two worlds without faltering.

Feeling the gulf between them widen, Jessie took a step backwards. Once she'd adored him. But that had been a long time ago. Now she didn't even know him. 'Look…' She cleared her throat. 'If you could just find me a pair of old jeans or something, that will be fine. Then I can get out of here and leave you to your life.'

Without responding, Silvio opened another cupboard and moments later he pushed several pieces of clothing into her arms. 'Try these. They should do until we can find you something else.'

Jessie looked down at the soft denim and nodded. 'This is perfect,' she said gruffly. 'I don't need anything else. I have stuff in my flat.' The thought of going back there left her cold with fear and he obviously had a similar reaction because his eyes hardened.

'Give me a list of the things you need and I'll send someone.'

Jessie shrank inwardly at the thought of anyone seeing how little she owned. 'There's no need. I have to go back anyway.'

'You're not going back, Jess. For the time being, you'll be living with me.'

Relief mingled with outrage and she wondered why being with this man triggered such contradictory emotions. 'Are you planning to keep me locked up here in your fancy bachelor pad just so that they can't get me?' Her laugh was high-pitched. 'That would cramp your style. I can just imagine what your new posh friends would say if they met me.'

'They'd like you. And if they didn't like you that would be their problem, not yours.'

Jessie turned away from him, staring into the wardrobe to hide the humiliating glitter of tears that she felt in her eyes. She must be tired, to be this close to crying. 'I can't stay here with you. It feels wrong.' She didn't add that she felt grubby and out of place. 'I need to leave now. I have to leave.' She said the words for her own benefit as much as his, trying to force herself to do the right thing. But nausea churned in her stomach at the thought of leaving. If she walked away from him, she'd be walking away from safety. *Did she really want to keep struggling and looking over her shoulder?*

'Don't waste time arguing with yourself.' Reading her mind, he strolled towards the door of the dressing room. 'You're not going anywhere, Jess. You're staying with me until I tell you it's safe for you to go back out there—and that's non-negotiable.'

Her eyes slid to his and she met his hard, unflinching gaze. He was being macho and over-protective and she knew she ought to argue with him. It horrified her to discover that she didn't want to.

Being protected felt good.

'Do you think they'll come after me?'

'I know they'll come after you. They're going to check that I told them the truth. But you don't need to be scared.' He spoke with the cool conviction of someone who'd never been scared of anything in his life. 'This place is a fortress. They can't get to you here.'

Something he'd said nagged at her brain. 'What do you

mean, they're going to check that you told them the truth? The truth about what? What did you say to them? Why did they back off?' Her heart rate was suddenly twice as fast and her palms were clammy as she recalled those terrifying moments in the alleyway. 'They shouldn't have let me go. I thought they were going to kill me—'

Tension rippled through his powerful frame and she wondered whether he'd always seemed this intimidating or whether she was just feeling more vulnerable than usual.

'Silvio? How did you persuade them not to?' Her mouth was suddenly dry and her limbs turned liquid. *'What did you say?'*

The silence stretched between them and he held her gaze, his dark eyes burning into hers. 'I told them the one thing guaranteed to ensure that no one touches you.' His tone had a raw, elemental edge and he studied her with brooding concentration. 'I told them you're my woman.'

CHAPTER THREE

'TELL me what you'd like to eat and my chef will cook it. Eggs? Bacon? Pancakes?'

'You told them I'm your woman. Why would you do that?' Jessie paced the length of his enormous living room, unable to focus on anything except what he'd just told her. 'I can't believe you did that.'

His woman…

Her stomach dropped because it was uncomfortably close to her adolescent fantasies. When other girls had been drooling over boy bands and football stars, Jessie had been thinking about Silvio Brianza. When she'd seen him with different women it had caused an almost physical pain and the depth of her misery had been intensified by the humiliating knowledge that he had been aware of her feelings.

She'd loved him until she'd ached, but he'd never treated her as anything other than his best friend's little sister.

They were separated by ten years and a gulf of experience.

And that gulf had been made even wider by the circumstances of her brother's death.

She was betraying him by even being here.

'Food, Jess,' he said patiently, and she glanced towards

him, too agitated to concentrate. Everything felt alien. The environment, him, even the clothes.

The jeans and the thin cashmere jumper fitted her perfectly but they felt like nothing she'd ever worn before.

It was amazing what money could buy.

'How can you think about food?' she said hoarsely. 'We need to talk about this!'

'We'll talk when you've eaten.' Maddeningly calm, Silvio turned to a woman who was hovering and spoke to her in Italian. Then he turned back to Jessie. 'She'll ask the chef to prepare something. You're too thin. When did you last eat?'

'I'm not thin, and, Silvio, we need to—'

'No, we don't need to do anything. You need to trust me.' He strolled towards the large glass table that was the focus of the far end of the enormous room. 'Come and join me.'

Torn between gnawing hunger and raging guilt, she didn't move.

'Sit, Jess.' His tone was neutral, as if he were bored with the entire situation. 'Or do you hate me so much you can't sit at my table?'

Jessie stared at him in silence, wondering how it was possible to feel so many things about one man. 'I can't sit at your table,' she said huskily, twisting the edge of the jumper with nervous fingers. 'I can't eat your food or sleep in your bed. I just can't. I know you saved me tonight, but that doesn't change the way I feel about you.'

His face revealed no emotion but his hand closed over the back of one chair, his knuckles white. 'So you'd rather starve yourself and put yourself at risk?'

'I can look after myself.'

He had the grace not to laugh. 'You need help, Jess.'

'I don't want help.'

'You mean you don't want help from *me*.' Dragging the

chair back from the table, he sat down, his eyes still fastened on her. His jaw was dark with stubble, his legs long and lean, and he looked like every woman's dark, forbidden fantasy.

'You're right,' Jessie croaked, registering the sudden weakening of her knees with a spasm of bitter regret. 'I don't want help from you. I don't want anything from you.'

Silvio reached out a hand and toyed with his fork, his movements slow and deliberate. 'If you leave this place tonight,' he said softly, 'they'll find you. Is that really what you want?'

Jessie rubbed her arms with her hands, trying to control the shivering. 'I can protect myself.'

'Like you did tonight? I'm not giving you a choice, Jess, so you don't need to stand there wondering whether you're betraying your brother's memory by eating at my table. It isn't your decision. If it makes you feel better you can tell yourself I'm holding you against your will.' A humourless smile tugged at the corners of his sensual mouth. 'Another crime to add to the many I've already committed against you.'

Dragging her eyes from his, Jessie looked at the window and thought about what was waiting for her out there in the darkness and the rain.

If she left him, she'd die and it was no use pretending otherwise.

He was the only one who could protect her against what was out there.

As if to undermine her resolve still further, at that moment several staff emerged and placed food on the table and her stomach gave an embarrassing rumble.

'You might as well eat while you're agonising over whether it's all right to accept my help.' Silvio gestured impatiently towards the table. 'Sit, Jess.'

The scent of fried bacon made her mouth water and she walked towards the table as hesitantly as a gazelle might approach a waterhole, knowing that a predator was watching.

Fortunately the table was large enough to allow dining without intimacy.

She pulled out the chair at the far end of the table from him. 'This place is huge.'

'Space is important to me.'

'Because of all those years cramped in one room?'

A shadow flickered across his face. 'Something like that.'

'Well, you've certainly left all that behind.' Curious in spite of herself, Jessie looked around her, momentarily distracted by what she saw. 'Did you build this?'

'Not with my bare hands, if that's what you're asking.' His low, masculine drawl was tinged with amusement. 'My company built it.'

It was impossible not to be impressed by what he'd achieved. 'You used to do it with your bare hands. You used to haul the bricks and sweat alongside the men.' Looking at the swell of muscle under the thin fabric of his expensive shirt, she wondered whether he still did. Something had to be responsible for his athletic physique and the raw power in those shoulders. That wasn't the body of a man who spent his days at a desk, pushing paper.

His next words confirmed her suspicions. 'I still do some of the physical work, but even I don't have time to erect entire apartment buildings and hotels single-handed. Are you going to eat standing up?'

Jessie sat on the edge of the chair. He obviously wasn't going to talk properly until she'd eaten, so she might as well eat. 'This company of yours—tell me what else you build.' She eyed the sleek glass table, wondering if it would crack if you put something heavy on it.

'Mostly hotels. But I can be persuaded to build corporate premises if the project interests me enough.'

Jessie lifted a knife in her hand and turned it, the silver catching the light and winking at her. Silver. 'You've come a long way from the building site.'

'That was the intention.'

'But you chose to build your fancy apartment block in the roughest part of London. You look out of your window every day and see what you left behind. A psychologist would say you were trying to prove something.'

'And an analyst would say it was a shrewd investment. It's a good position. In less than three years this has become the trendiest place to live in the city.' He spoke with the confidence of someone whose judgements had proved unerring. 'Right by the river. Close to the commercial heart of London.'

'Uncomfortably close to the rough part of London.'

'This is a cosmopolitan city.' Silvio sat back in his chair as a chef dressed in white placed more food in the middle of the table. *'Grazie, Roberto.'* He spoke a few words of Italian and the man melted away, leaving them alone again.

Determined not to show how impressed she was, Jessie stifled a laugh. 'Does that guy stay up all night in case you want to eat?'

'I have a team of chefs. They work a rota.'

'You're so rich now you can't boil yourself an egg?'

'I entertain a lot. Generally my guests expect more than a boiled egg.'

'But tonight you're slumming it. Stuck with me. Poor you.' Hiding her self-consciousness behind bravado, Jessie leaned forward and lifted the lid from one of the plates. 'Mmm. Bacon.' Seduced by the delicious smell, she suddenly realised how hungry she was. 'Can I help myself or does someone have to serve me?'

'I thought you'd rather have privacy.'

In other words he was embarrassed by her. Jessie's face flamed and she stabbed her fork into a few rashers of bacon, telling herself that she didn't care what he thought. 'Don't you want any?'

'Not at the moment.' Silvio poured himself a black coffee. 'I'm not hungry.'

'I'm always hungry.' Forgetting that she was trying to be reserved with him, Jessie looked at the bacon on her plate and wondered if she'd taken too much. Deciding that it would draw more attention to herself to put some of it back, she sat there awkwardly.

'Is that all you're going to eat?' Silvio stood up and strolled round the table. Without asking for her input, he piled more bacon on her plate and then added a heap of fluffy scrambled eggs and warm, fresh rolls. 'If you don't eat it, you'll offend my chef and I can't afford to lose him. He's too good at his job.'

Nibbling the corner of the most delicious roll she'd ever tasted, Jessie had to agree with him. 'He cooks like this for you every day?' She savoured the scrambled eggs, moaning with pleasure. 'Is he married? Does he want to be?'

He ignored her question. 'When you've finished eating you should try and get some more sleep. Tomorrow I'll take you shopping.' He was back at his end of the table, topping up his coffee.

Her mouth now full of hot bacon, Jessie stopped chewing and stared at him. Then she swallowed hard. 'Shopping?' She started to laugh because the idea was ridiculous. 'You're mixing me up with some other girl, Silvio. I don't need new clothes—I need a new life, and you can't buy that from Harvey Nichols. And anyway…' without thinking, she picked up a piece of crispy bacon in her fingers and nibbled it '…I don't have any spare money for shopping.'

'You'll be spending my money.'

Noticing the napkin next to her plate, Jessie started to wipe her fingers and immediately smeared grease on the crisp, clean linen. Mortified, she considered trying to hide it but then realised that he was watching her. Her face scarlet, she shifted in her chair. 'Sorry. I wasn't concentrating. I picked the bacon up.' Jessie clutched the napkin self-consciously. 'I'll wash it if you show me where.'

Astonishment lit his dark eyes. 'Just leave it. Someone else will do it. Why would you even suggest it?'

She gave a hollow laugh and put the napkin carefully on the table. 'Because I'm usually that someone else.'

He registered that comment with a slight hardening of his jaw. 'Well, all that is going to change. Your life is going to change.'

Suddenly she didn't feel like eating any more. 'You think if you throw money at me, it will solve the problem?'

Her eyes lifted to his and they stared at each other in tense silence.

'It will solve at least part of the problem.'

'Money won't change the way I feel about you and, anyway, I don't need your money. I can earn my own.' Seeing the flare of disapproval in his eyes, she sighed. Even though she knew the truth, it didn't feel good knowing that he thought that about her. 'Look—there's something I need to tell you—'

'Forget it. I don't want to know.' His tone was clipped. 'What I do want to know is why you were paying off Johnny's debts.'

Hearing his name knocked the breath from her body and Jessie sank her teeth into her lower lip, appalled by the sudden slug of emotion that hit her. 'Don't say his name.'

'Why?'

'Because I—I can't—Just don't!' She was out of her chair,

heart racing, the breath trapped in her throat, the food on her plate forgotten.

'You're paying for his mistakes, Jess,' Silvio said, his voice low and savage. 'It has to stop.'

'It will stop when I've paid the money he owed.'

'They want more than money from you, *tesoro*.'

The endearment cut right through to her heart. She didn't want endearments. She didn't want anything from him. 'I know.' Jessie started to pace again, feeling trapped in a situation not of her making. 'I know what they want.' And the knowledge had kept her awake every night for months.

'*Maledezione*, every man who looks at you wants the same thing.' He was out of his chair too, his tone thickened with anger, his hand slicing through the air. 'Do you know what those men in the bar were thinking? Every last one of them was imagining you naked and thanks to your choice of dress, it didn't take much imagination.'

'Joe insists that his singers dress like that.'

'Because the women he employs provide services other than their voices!' He dragged his fingers through his hair, his beautiful features set and hard, power and authority stamped in every line of his handsome face. 'I can't believe you'd do that to yourself, Jess.'

'What I do with my life is none of your business.'

'It's just become my business.' He was unyielding and remorseless. 'Why are you wasting your incredible voice in a place like that? You could be working anywhere.'

Jessie looked down at herself—at her borrowed clothes—and gave a cynical smile. 'I'm a nightclub singer, Silvio.'

'No. You're a singer. It was your decision to use your voice in a nightclub. There are other choices.'

'Not for people like me.' She told herself that it was his height and build that made him seem intimidating.

'Jess…' He spoke her name through his teeth, as if he was struggling not to ignite. 'Your voice is exceptional. Truly exceptional. With training, you could go right to the top. You'd be an international star.'

Jess was still for a moment, immobilised by the vision he'd painted. And then she remembered that dreams had a way of crumbling. 'Hard to be an international star without a passport,' she said flippantly, and Silvio made an impatient sound in his throat.

'So it's better to just give up, is that right?'

She swallowed. Not to anyone would she confess that when she sang, she wasn't in a seedy club. She was up there, singing for an enraptured crowd of thousands. 'Sometimes dreaming can make things worse.'

'Dreaming can drive you forwards.'

'Dreaming can emphasise the gap between hopes and reality.'

'Then make the dream your reality!' His eyes were two dangerous slits and Jessie looked at him uncertainly, shaken by the barely leashed anger she sensed in him.

'I don't understand why you're so upset.'

'I don't understand why you're not *more* upset,' he countered in an aggressive tone. 'Don't you ever feel angry with Johnny for leaving you in this situation?'

Jessie blinked rapidly, her hands balled into fists. 'Yes,' she whispered. 'Sometimes I feel angry. And then I feel guilty, because I know a lot of it was my fault.'

Silvio's face hardened. 'None of it was your fault.'

'You're wrong.' The words clogged her throat. She was torn between the urge to confide in him and the urge to walk away. 'There was so much more I could have done. I made mistakes.'

'We all made mistakes,' Silvio said dismissively, unconsciously demonstrating the blistering confidence that had helped earn him millions. 'And Johnny made the most mistakes of all.'

'You have no right to blame him.'

'I have every right.' He prowled over to the window, turning his back to her, everything about him screaming tension. 'He was selfish and weak and he should have taken better care of you. He behaved like a boy when he should have stood up and been a man.'

'Well, not everyone is as tough as you are!' She flung that observation at his back and saw his powerful shoulders tense.

'You're in this situation because of him. If I hadn't come tonight—' The words were cut off abruptly and he turned suddenly. 'It ends now, Jessie, this life of yours. Let's stop pretending you have a million options to choose from.'

She was frozen to the spot by his words. 'You're blaming Johnny for everything,' she whispered, 'just because he isn't here to defend himself.'

'I wish he were here.' Silvio gave a vicious growl, his thick, dark lashes framing blazing eyes. 'One of the things I regret most is that I didn't make him face up to the truth.'

Jessie felt the colour drain from her face. 'You were supposed to be his friend.'

'If I'd been a better friend I would have forced him to remember his responsibilities instead of giving him what he asked for. I failed him. And do I regret that?' His tone held the bitter notes of self-recrimination. 'Yes, I do. More than you will ever know. But there's something I regret even more than that, and that's not reminding him of his duty to you. He should have protected you!'

'He loved me.' Instinctively leaping to her brother's defence, Jessie backed away. 'Johnny loved me.'

'*Sì*, he loved you.' Silvio's tone was contemptuous. 'He

loved you the way that suited him, not the way that was best for you. But all that is going to change. You're not going back to that life, Jess. It's over. I should not have left you alone and from now on I'm doing what your brother should have done. I'm taking you away from that place. And if being with me makes you feel guilty, deal with it.' He was merciless and un-yielding and Jessie backed away a few more steps, her heart pounding.

'I'm not your responsibility. I don't want your help. I hate you.' She glanced around the sumptuous apartment, feeling disloyal to Johnny just by being there. The contrast between this and the desolate place where he'd spent his last few hours was painful to think about. 'Why would you even want to help me, knowing the way I feel about you?'

A muscle flickered in his lean cheek. 'You lost your brother. I don't blame you for the things you feel about me.'

It was emotion, and Silvio Brianza didn't do emotion.

'Well, I blame you, Silvio!' Her voice shook with enough passion for both of them. 'You gave him the money. Without that he wouldn't have been able to do it.'

His eyes darkened and he seemed about to say something, but then changed his mind. 'I know what I did.' His tone was flat. Neutral. He made no attempt to dodge her accusations or excuse himself. 'And I know you blame me.'

'Is that why you're helping me? Guilt? I thought you never looked back. I thought you always look forward.'

He took so long to answer that she wondered if he'd heard her question.

And then he inhaled slowly. 'I've already lost him,' he breathed. 'I won't lose you, too. That's looking forward.'

His words sent a shiver of awareness through her body and a deep, heavy sadness because she knew they'd lost each other years before.

It was all too late. The blame and recrimination had eroded their relationship as surely as the weather eroded rock. It had been reshaped into something she no longer recognised.

'I can't pretend to be…' it was difficult to say the words '…your woman.'

'Yes, you can. Johnny would have wanted you to do whatever it took to keep yourself safe.'

Jessie's heart was pounding against her chest. 'So you're going to move me into your fancy apartment, dress me up in some shiny new clothes and kiss me in public, is that it?'

'You'll go where I go.' His eyes dropped to her mouth. 'And I'll kiss you when I want to kiss you.' He was self-assured, strong and more of a man than anyone else she'd ever met.

And the mention of kissing knocked the strength from her knees. 'It's a crazy plan.'

'What's crazy about it?'

'Well, for a start your current girlfriend is likely to object that you've moved some lowlife into your apartment.'

'Don't speak about yourself like that. And—I'm not in a relationship at the moment.'

Jessie looked at him in disbelief. 'Oh, sure. A man like you must really have to scrabble around for a date. I'm not naïve, Silvio. Women have always found you irresistible. I know you get thousands of offers.'

He didn't smile. 'Just because I have the opportunity to sleep with a woman, it doesn't mean I do,' he said softly, his words a subtle condemnation of the life he believed she led. 'I've always been extremely selective.'

Jessie looked at him warily and then glanced around her. Nothing but the best for Silvio Brianza. Apartment, car—*women*. 'All the more reason why no one is going to believe I'm your woman. I wouldn't be convincing. I don't know how to live in this world.'

'This world is easy.' His wry tone was tinged with humour. 'It's yours that's the hard place to live.'

'Life is hard, Silvio. That's how it goes.' She twisted the ends of her hair, aware that it had dried fluffy. 'And how long do we keep this charade up for?'

'Until I say it can stop.'

Jessie looked at him in exasperation. 'They'll never believe you. No woman involved with you would work in a seedy bar.'

Silvio gave a grim smile. 'You no longer have that job.'

'You lost me my job?'

'You don't need a job that requires you to dress like the centrefold of a pornographic magazine.'

'It paid well!'

'For all the wrong reasons. You're not going back there.' His voice harsh, he made it clear that there was no room for negotiation on that point.

Outraged and suddenly frightened, Jessie paced across the pale wooden floor. 'You shouldn't have done that, Silvio.'

'Did you love the job that much?'

She stopped pacing and stared straight ahead of her. 'No,' she croaked. 'No, of course I didn't. But I don't want you taking control of my life! How am I supposed to earn money? How am I supposed to pay them back? And whether or not we go ahead with this charade you're proposing, I'm going to need a job when it finishes.'

'I'll give you a job.'

Jessie glared at him. 'I don't want your charity.'

'It isn't charity. It's employment.'

'How can you offer me a job?' Fraught and exhausted, Jessie gave a hysterical laugh. 'You build hotels.'

'Once they're built, my hotels are run by a team of people. Live music is one of the entertainments we offer.'

'You're offering me a job as a singer?'

'I'm certainly not expecting you to lift bricks.'

Pride warred with practicality. She wanted to tell him she'd rather die than accept a job from him. The problem was, if she didn't accept it, dying might well be her fate.

She stood still, aware of his unwavering scrutiny, knowing that this was a turning point for her. She had to make a decision.

Her survival instincts proved stronger than her principles.

It wasn't really charity, was it, if he was paying her to do a job?

And the opportunity to move away, somewhere miles from here, was too tempting to reject out of hand.

'Where would I go?'

'To start with, Sicily. My flagship hotel opened last month and we're hosting the celebrity wedding of the year in a few days' time. Gisella Howard is marrying Brentwood Altingham the Third.' The name brought a faint smile to his hard mouth. 'Old money. Very old money.'

Trying not to look impressed, Jessie shrugged. 'Do they know you were from the streets?'

'That's why they've chosen my hotel.' His eyes gleamed with irony. 'They're confident I can handle security.'

And they were right, Jessie thought, remembering the bold, fearless way he'd extracted her from danger. 'And you've employed all your dangerous friends to keep the paparazzi at a distance.'

'Something like that.'

'So you're offering me a job in a super-smart hotel?' Impossibly daunted, Jessie suddenly wished she had the confidence to take it. 'I'm really going to fit in there wearing my gold dress.'

'You won't be wearing your gold dress. And it's not open

to negotiation.' Silvio glanced at his Rolex. 'It's really late. You're obviously exhausted so go and get some rest. Do me a favour and don't try and escape because my team have instructions not to let you pass. Use my room. I'll take one of the others. I have to go out for a while.'

'Go out?'

He was leaving her?

The warm cocoon of safety that had surrounded her since she'd slammed into him in the alley evaporated and suddenly she wanted to beg him not to go. 'W-where are you going?'

'Out.' Without elaborating, he strode towards the door, leaving Jessie immobilised with panic.

What was so urgent that he had to go out in the middle of the night?

And how was she going to keep herself safe without him?

'Silvio…' Her tone was urgent and he turned, a frown in his eyes, his mind clearly on something else.

'What?'

Jessie tried to ask him not to go. Her mouth opened but the words wouldn't come. What was the matter with her? Why was she being so pathetic? 'Nothing,' she croaked finally. 'I'll see you.' It required a monumental effort to hide how bad she felt, and for a moment she thought she'd failed because he stared at her, his gaze sharpening.

'*Non ti preoccupare.* Don't worry. You're safe here, Jess. This place has state-of-the-art security.'

'I'm not worried.' She snapped the words, hating herself for showing her insecurities and reminding herself that she'd been coping on her own for the past three years. Watching her own back.

But in the last few hours she'd tasted safety and she didn't want to let it go. After three years of sleeping with one eye open and living her life on a knife edge, she'd suddenly been able to relax, safe in the knowledge that he was the one in control.

Aware that he was still watching her closely, Jessie managed a casual shrug. 'Have fun.' Where else would he be going at this time of night but to see a woman? And why should that thought make her feel so miserable?

Silvio checked his watch again. 'Get to bed, Jessie.' As the door clicked shut behind him, Jessie flinched.

Suddenly she was aware of the enormous space around her and felt terrifyingly vulnerable. Looking around her, she wondered what he meant by 'state-of-the-art security'. Presumably not her, holding a saucepan, ready to bash an intruder.

How were you supposed to know if anyone was lying in wait in a place like this?

It was full of dark, hidden spaces.

Having worked herself into a panic, Jessie tried telling herself that any apartment he'd built was bound to be secure but she knew it wasn't the building that had provided that security blanket.

It had been the man.

And he'd gone.

It was hours later when Silvio arrived back at the apartment.

Grimly satisfied with what he'd achieved, he dismissed the hovering staff and poured himself a drink.

As the first streaks of dawn split the night sky, he stared sightlessly through the glass, trying not to think what would have happened to her if he hadn't chosen to return when he had. What he'd learned about her life over the past few hours had turned his insides ice cold.

He'd asked questions, called in favours, exploited contacts, all the time spreading the same message:

That Jessie was his and no other man's.

He'd been unable to think of any other way of ensuring her protection.

Draining his drink in a single mouthful, he reflected on the irony of the situation.

It was a good job that both of them were private people, he thought grimly as he stared into his empty glass, otherwise everyone would know that an emotional involvement between the two of them was impossible.

The apartment was silent as he walked towards one of the guest suites but he paused outside the master bedroom, unable to resist the impulse to check on her.

Opening the door quietly, he looked at the bed and saw it empty.

There was no sign of her.

Preparing to fire his head of security, Silvio was about to leave the room and create hell when he noticed that the velvet throw from the bed was missing. Frowning, he strolled into the room, a suspicion forming in his mind.

He checked the bathroom and then moved across to the dressing room. It was in darkness. Rubbing his hand over the back of his neck, he stilled for a moment and tried to think like her.

Her childhood fear of being trapped had never left her and he hadn't needed to witness her performance earlier to know how much she hated being on the top floor. A penthouse to Jessie wasn't real-estate heaven—it was hell. Knowing that, he also knew that there was no way she'd shut herself in a dressing room.

Turning his head, Silvio narrowed his eyes and rejected the possibility that flew into his head.

No, she wouldn't—

Or maybe she would.

Silently, he moved through the bedroom and paused outside the door that concealed the escape slide. It was open a crack and he slid his fingers into the gap and widened it.

Jessie lay curled up on the floor only centimetres away from the top of the slide, her slender body swamped by the huge throw from the bed, her arm flung protectively over the shoebox.

Silvio stared down at her in silence, a thousand emotions rushing through his head.

What terror inhabited her mind that she'd rather sleep in the bottom of a cupboard than in his comfortable bed? His apartment was protected by the most sophisticated security in existence, but Jessie hadn't trusted it.

He saw the faint smudge of make-up under her eyes and realised that she'd been crying.

The fact that she'd waited for privacy before she'd allowed herself to cry created more strain on his conscience.

She hadn't wanted to break down in front of him and he should be grateful for that, shouldn't he? He knew nothing about offering comfort to a woman and all he'd ever done to Jessie was hurt her.

Lifting her easily, he carried her back to the bed and her eyes opened. Her lids were heavy, her eyes glazed with sleep.

'Silvio—'

'Go back to sleep.' The taste of regret made his voice gruff and he lowered her to the mattress and tucked the throw around her. Was she going to beg him to put her back in the escape chute?

But she didn't.

Instead, her hand slid into his and Silvio tensed because it was so unlike Jessie to show weakness and he had no idea how he was supposed to respond. Ordinarily he was the last man to whom she would turn for comfort and the fact that she had reached for his hand told him that she must be desperate.

Without breathing, he looked down at their joined hands—saw the fragility of her pale, delicate fingers placed trustingly in his strong palm. After a moment's hesitation he closed his fingers over hers and Jessie sighed softly.

'I'm glad you're home,' she said sleepily, a smile hovering around her mouth as her eyes drifted shut again. 'Are you going out again?'

Knowing that if she'd been fully awake she would have consigned him to hell, Silvio found it difficult to speak. 'No,' he said finally, his voice rough around the edges, 'no, I'm not going anywhere, *tesoro*. You can sleep now.'

And she did. With the smile still on her face and her hand locked in his.

Trapped there, Silvio found himself forced to confront issues he didn't want to confront.

Like the dangerous chemistry that drew them together.

And the fact that because of him, she'd lost the most important thing in her life.

Silvio stared down at her pale face and narrow shoulders and at the battered shoebox that she was gripping like a lifeline.

He wanted to open it to see what it was that she refused to be parted from, but he didn't want to risk waking her. Neither did he want to intrude on her privacy because he knew how much that mattered to her.

The resolve hardened inside him.

He couldn't undo what had been done. He couldn't bring back her brother.

But he could take her away from the life she'd fallen into.

He could take her away from this hell that was all she thought she deserved, and give her something different.

He owed her that.

CHAPTER FOUR

'You don't have to take me shopping.' It was another blow to her badly damaged pride that he'd suggested it. 'It's a luxury I can't afford.'

'You need clothes,' Silvio said smoothly. 'It isn't a luxury, it's a necessity.'

Unable to argue with that, Jessie shrank lower in the passenger seat of his Ferrari, averting her eyes from the stares. She felt as though everyone was a witness to her humiliation. 'Just a couple of things, then. Maybe another pair of jeans. Do you have to drive this car? Everyone is looking.'

But she knew that the driver was every bit as conspicuous as his car. With his Mediterranean good looks and spectacular physique, Silvio drew covetous glances wherever he went.

'You would have preferred a chauffeur-driven limousine?' He pulled the car up on a double yellow line outside the most exclusive store in Knightsbridge and a uniformed man immediately sprang forward.

'Mr Brianza.' His voice oozed awe and respect and Silvio tossed him the keys and said something that Jessie didn't catch.

'I don't think they sell my sort of clothes here.' Stepping cautiously onto the pavement, she glanced around her furtively, daunted by the throng of beautifully groomed women who strode past her in tailored skirts and vertiginous heels, all of them brimming with confidence. Gazing at one woman's perfect straight hair, she fingered her tumbled dark curls self-consciously and then stiffened as Silvio took her arm.

'Try not to look as though you're expecting someone to assault you,' he said mildly, guiding her towards the glass doors with a purposeful stride. 'You're with me now. No one is going to touch you.'

He was touching her, and the feel of his hand on her arm and the brush of his body against hers created a lethal assault on her senses that was as unwelcome as her disturbingly clear memories of nestling against him while she'd slept.

Instead of pushing him away and telling him she didn't need him, she'd clung to his hand as a drowning man might have clung to a floating object in a raging river.

He hadn't mentioned what had happened, but she'd thought about nothing else. Although she'd been alone in the bed when she'd woken up, she knew he'd stayed beside her for the rest of the night.

Something else she was supposed to feel grateful for, Jessie thought moodily, staring in disbelief at the perfect arch of a woman's eyebrows as she hurried past on her way to somewhere important. Her image of him as a cold-hearted monster was becoming uncomfortably distorted.

Cringing at the memory of how frightened she'd been once he'd left the flat, Jessie scolded herself silently. She was pathetic. She just hoped his fancy apartment didn't have CCTV or he'd be treated to some embarrassing footage of her checking under the bed and inside the wardrobes before finally allowing herself to sleep.

As Silvio guided her into a lift Jessie stared in front of her, determined not to look at the mirrored walls. She knew what she'd see. A woman who wasn't supposed to be there.

'I've been thinking about this suggestion of yours.'

'The one where you get to stay alive?' His gaze flickered to hers, his dark eyes so compelling that it was impossible to look away.

'It isn't that simple.' With effort she averted her gaze and sucked in some air. 'I need to pay back the rest of the money Johnny owed them or this is never going to end. You said you'd give me a job, which is great, but I'm still not going to earn it fast enough.' She had to force the words through the tiny chink in her pride. 'I know you have contacts—I wondered if you knew anyone I could go to for a loan. I think it would be safer to owe money to a stranger.'

'You don't owe money to anyone.' Silvio pressed a button on the lift. 'I've repaid the debt.'

'You paid them?' Shocked, Jessie turned to look at him. 'When?'

'Last night.'

Last night, when he'd left her alone. Stunned, it took her a moment to respond. 'I didn't want you to do that. I was paying them myself—'

'Piece by piece,' he drawled contemptuously, his disparaging glance surprisingly hurtful.

It was obvious that she couldn't sink any lower in his opinion, and Jessie wondered why that should matter to her.

She wasn't supposed to care what he thought, was she?

Feeling the humiliating sting of tears behind her eyes, Jessie lifted her chin. 'I will pay you back.'

'I'll speak to my finance department and they can work something out.' Silvio dismissed the subject as if it were nothing and she stood stiffly, slowly digesting the fact that the debt was finally paid.

All those years of worry. Years of slog, terror and sheer bone-numbing exhaustion.

She felt as though a heavy object had finally been lifted away from her.

She just wished that he hadn't been the one who had lifted it.

Why had he done that?

'Thank you,' she said huskily, finally managing to say the words. *She'd never thought she'd be thanking him for anything.* 'I—I don't understand why you bothered bringing me here in that case. You don't have to go to all this trouble.' The lift doors opened and she reached out to press the button for the ground floor.

'*Maledezione*, what are you doing?' His hand closed over hers and he intercepted her movement.

'You said you'd paid off the debt.' This close to his body it was hard to breathe and Jessica's face flamed as she felt the now embarrassingly familiar burn low in her pelvis. 'It's over.'

'It isn't over,' he growled. 'Come on, Jess. You're not that naïve. The money was only part of what they wanted from you and you know it.'

She did know it.

And the knowledge had terrified her. The thought of stepping out there again had terrified her. Every night she'd wondered whether this was going to be the night they won.

'You're right, of course.' Her voice was calmer than it should have been. 'I'd like my knife back.'

'I have no intention of giving you the knife. If they'd found that they would have used it on you. The only way to stop them claiming what they want is for them to think you're with me. At the moment they do think that. As long as we don't give them any reason to doubt it, you'll be safe.'

Feeling intensely vulnerable, Jessica stared at the centre of his chest. 'So basically the choice is that I take my chances with them, or I take my chances with you.'

'I'm not dangerous. '

It was such a manifestly false statement that Jessica laughed, but it was a hysterical laugh, devoid of humour. 'Make up your mind. Last night you told me you were dangerous too.'

'All right, let me put that another way.' A sardonic smile touched his beautiful mouth. 'I'm not dangerous to you.'

Oh, but he was.

She knew that this one man had the power to do her more damage than every gang prowling the streets of London.

And he knew it.

He'd always known how she felt about him.

Jessie drew in a shuddering breath, reminding herself that everything was different now. He wasn't her hero any more. He was strong, yes. And powerful. But he wasn't the saint she'd once thought he was.

Her eyes were open wide and her heart was safely shut away.

He couldn't hurt her any more than he already had, could he?

And it would be crazy to refuse his protection. She'd lived her life on the edge for long enough to know that when help offered itself, you took it. 'I don't think it will work,' she said huskily. 'They're going to know I'm not the sort of woman who is usually in your life. I don't go to film premieres and celebrity parties. I don't know how to walk down a red carpet.'

'You put one leg in front of the other,' Silvio drawled. 'And celebrity parties and film premieres are going to seem like a holiday after the life you've been leading. It isn't something you need to practise.'

The lift doors opened but Jessie didn't move, daunted by the acres of glass and the sheer elegance of the building. 'I don't know how to shop in places like this.'

'That's easy too.' His hand closed over her wrist and he urged her forwards. 'You just find something you like and you buy it. It's not rocket science.'

'I don't like spending your money.'

'Now, that's something no woman has said to me before.' His smile was shockingly appealing. 'You're missing an opportunity for revenge, Jess. This is your chance to fleece me.' With his usual cool confidence, he walked towards a woman who was waiting. 'Alternatively you could consider it a necessary investment on the part of your employer. You're singing at the most important society wedding of the decade. You need to look the part.'

And that was another thing. It was all very well singing in Joe's Bar, but another thing entirely to sing in front of a discerning audience.

Just the thought of it made her stomach cramp with nerves.

What would they want her to sing?

What if they hated her voice?

Guided into an elegantly furnished private room, Jessie sat on a low, comfortable sofa and watched as clothes were modelled for her by a series of haughty models with endless legs.

She sat stiffly, feeling horribly out of place and painfully conscious of what they must be thinking about her.

After ten minutes of smiling politely, she turned to Silvio. 'I'm not sure what I'm doing here. Am I supposed to clap?'

'You make a note of the ones you like.' Preoccupied with answering emails, Silvio's eyes were fixed on the screen of his BlackBerry. 'Then you try them on. After that you take them home and wear them. Simple.'

He thought that was simple?

At the moment it felt like one of the hardest things she'd ever done.

Her confidence didn't increase when she turned back to the private fashion show in time to see a model staring hungrily at Silvio. She was sleek, glamorous and confident and Jessie suddenly wondered what on earth had possessed him to think he could convincingly pass her off as his woman.

'It doesn't matter how you dress me,' she mumbled, fiddling with the ends of her hair, 'I'm not going to look like her. I don't know why you're bothering.'

Silvio lifted his gaze and frowned. 'I wouldn't want you to look like her,' he murmured in an undertone. 'She's extremely bony.'

'You're kidding, right?' Jessica's eyes widened as she watched the girl disappear behind the curtain. 'She's beautiful. And confident.'

'Confidence is an act.' Silvio glanced at Jessie's face, exasperation gleaming in his eyes. 'Jess, what is the matter with you? You faced a bunch of thugs in an alleyway but here you are looking at a few fancy clothes and you're scared?'

Jessie bristled defensively. 'I didn't say I was scared,' she said fiercely. 'A bunch of posh clothes don't worry me.' But she was saying it to convince herself as much as him, and perhaps he realised that because his eyes narrowed.

'I understood that choosing a new wardrobe was most women's idea of paradise.'

'The women you mix with, maybe.'

Women who were nothing like her.

She tried to imagine what it must be like to have nothing more serious to worry about than what you were going to wear.

'Maybe I haven't got used to the idea that I can actually

have any of this stuff.' She shrugged awkwardly, reluctant to reveal how inadequate the whole thing made her feel, or how intimidating she found the groomed perfection of the models. 'Maybe it's just seeing it modelled.'

'That seemed to be the best way for you to see the clothes.' He stretched out his legs and Jessie wished she could be even a fraction as relaxed as he was.

'I can see how the clothes look on them, but not on me.' Couldn't he see the difference? 'We're not the same shape, for a start.'

'So what do you want?'

Her face scarlet, Jessie gnawed her lip, wishing she could just melt into the sofa and disappear. 'I don't know. Can I just try them on myself—with no one watching?'

'No, because I don't want any repeats of the gold dress. But I'll agree on a compromise. You can model them for me. I'll decide.' He gestured to the woman masterminding the fashion show and moments later the room was empty and they were alone. 'The clothes are all on rails behind the curtains. Help yourself. If anything doesn't fit, let me know and they'll bring a different size.'

Her face burning from his derogatory comments about her gold dress, Jessie looked at the expensive cut of his trousers and decided that being hard up was probably nothing more than a distant memory for him.

'What's it like,' she blurted out, 'to be able to buy anything you want without thinking about how much it costs? Does it feel weird?'

'You tell me,' he drawled softly, and Jessie realised with a flash of disbelief that he was giving her free rein to buy anything she wanted.

For a moment she didn't move, waiting for him to laugh and name a budget she had to work within, but his attention was back on his BlackBerry, his long fingers flying over the keys as he dealt with another email.

'Right—I'll just try something on…' Relieved that he didn't appear to be paying attention, Jessie stepped onto the stage, wincing as her cheap trainers squeaked.

Suddenly realising how ridiculous she must look, she giggled and turned to face him. 'And here we have Jessie, modelling this season's latest just-pulled-through-a-hedge look—' she pushed her hand into her hair and pouted dramatically '—in last season's jeans and jumper…' Her eyes met his and his gaze was thoughtful.

'It's good to see you laughing again.'

Laughing?

Oh, God, she was laughing—for the first time in as long as she could remember. And with *him*.

What was the matter with her?

Buying these clothes was a life-saving necessity, not a frivolous spending spree. She was doing this because she had to, not because she wanted to.

She wasn't supposed to be enjoying herself.

Jessie's smile faded and she backed towards the curtain. 'I—I'll go and try on the rest of those clothes.' Horrified with herself, she took refuge behind the curtains, her mouth dry and her heart pounding.

This was what happened when you were forced to accept help from your enemy. When the person you hated became your protector, you were in bigger trouble than ever before.

Jessie looked at the rails of clothes.

She didn't want to take anything from him but she needed clothes so that she could do the wretched job he was offering her. She couldn't sing for Mr and Mrs Celebrity couple without looking the part.

His words stuck in her head. *I don't want any repeats of the gold dress.*

He thought she had no fashion sense.

Thinking about how hard it had been even to keep herself clothed on her non-existent budget, Jessie glared at the clothes as if they were responsible for her situation.

She'd show him fashion sense.

Her attention caught by a shimmer of peacock blue, she reached out and snatched the dress from its hanger. Seeing the label, she gave a gulp and almost put it straight back. A dress like this would cost a fortune. More than she earned in a year, including tips.

But where was the harm in trying it on?

Too much of a woman to resist the temptation, she wriggled out of her jeans.

As soon as the delicate fabric whispered over her skin, she gave a low moan of appreciation. She didn't need a mirror to know that it was going to look good. This dress would look good on anyone.

Taking a pair of shoes from the selection that had been left out for her, Jessie slid them on, noting how much more comfortable they were than the cheap budget-store version she crammed her feet into every night.

'Goodbye, blisters,' she muttered, pushing back the curtain and stepping onto the catwalk. Hoping she wasn't going to fall flat on her face, she strolled forward, imitating the swaying confident walk of the models. 'This store is trying to fleece you,' she said lightly. 'There's nothing but expensive stuff back here.'

'That's good.' In the middle of reading an email, Silvio didn't even glance up and Jessie felt a rush of anticlimax, thrown by the fact he hadn't even looked at her.

'Did you hear what I said? They're trying to make you spend loads.'

'I heard you.'

'Well, you at least ought to tell me if you think it's worth the money.'

His glance was so fleeting that she almost missed it. 'You look fine.'

That was it? *That was all he was going to say?*

'At that price it ought to be more than fine.' Curiously deflated by his indifferent response, Jessie was about to turn away when she noticed the tension in his shoulders. Puzzled, she glanced at his face but his eyes were on the screen in his hand. 'Why did you come here if you're too busy for this?'

'I'm not too busy.'

'Well, you're obviously really stressed about something. So what's on your mind? What is there to worry about now that you're rich?'

Finally he looked at her.

Self-conscious under his penetrating dark gaze, Jessie shifted awkwardly. 'What? There's no mirror so I couldn't look at myself. Am I wearing it the wrong way round or something? Is there something wrong with it? You said it was fine.'

It was a moment before he answered and when he did his voice was terse. 'There's nothing wrong with it. And this is going to take all day if we spend this long on each outfit.' He returned his attention to his phone and Jessie felt a rush of humiliation, all too aware that he'd paid the model more attention than he'd paid her.

Infuriated with herself for minding, she scowled at him. 'I can't pick a whole wardrobe from the stuff back there,' she said huskily, horrified to discover that she had a lump in her throat. 'It's all really expensive.'

'It doesn't matter what it costs.'

'Do you throw money at every problem you encounter?'

The words fell out of her mouth without the approval of her brain. 'Because you ought to know that spending money on me isn't going to change the way I feel about you, so if that's why you're doing this, you shouldn't waste your money.'

His fingers stilled on the keys. 'If a problem can be solved with money, then I use money. You have no clothes that fit your new life, so I'm solving that problem.' His response to her impassioned outburst was supremely logical. 'And I don't expect it to change the way you feel about me.'

'Good, because it doesn't.' She wondered why she suddenly felt ungrateful. 'But I'd rather not be in debt to you for the rest of my life if you don't mind. So could you snap your fingers or whatever it is you do when you want attention, and ask them to bring something in a more realistic price range? Tell them I want normal-person clothes. The sort I can wear around the supermarket.'

'You won't be going anywhere near a supermarket for the foreseeable future. And they've chosen well.' His gaze lingered on the dress. 'It's perfect for the role you'll be playing.'

He was reminding her that this was a role. That none of this was real.

That she wasn't dressing up for him.

He didn't want her getting the wrong idea.

Brought back down to earth with a hard bump, Jessie swallowed. She hadn't for one moment forgotten that, had she? She hadn't started to think this was real? It was an escape from her old life. A way out.

Temporary.

No matter how devastating he was to look at, no matter how masculine and self-possessed, he was still the man who was ultimately responsible for her brother's death. There never could be anything between them.

She squared her shoulders, her spine stiff. 'Well, if you want me to dress for the 'role' then you'd better tell me what you have planned. Where are we going?'

'This afternoon we're flying to Sicily. I'm hosting a champagne reception on my yacht—I want you by my side. And there will be numerous other events that we're expected to attend. The clothes are a gift, Jessie. Accept the gift.' A cynical smile played around his sexy mouth. 'Despite what you seem to think, you're not going to bankrupt me in one shopping trip.'

'Events? What events? I thought you were employing me to sing.'

'I am. You'll sing at the wedding at the end of the week. After that we'll work out a more permanent contract.'

Jessie fiddled with the dress, daunted by what he'd just said. 'You're hosting a champagne reception? I won't know anyone.'

'You will by the end of the evening.'

'What if no one talks to me?'

He lifted an eyebrow, his eyes perplexed. 'Why wouldn't they talk to you?'

'I'm not like them.'

'You've never met them, so you can't know that.' Clearly at a loss to understand her qualms, Silvio gave a frown of irritation. 'You should have more confidence in yourself.'

'Well, I haven't,' Jessie said flatly, 'and I bet you I'll be standing on my own all night. We're not all as confident as you! Even when you were living in care and your only possession was your fists, you were still confident. How did you do that?'

'Because I've never believed that a person's intrinsic worth comes from what they can buy.' Slipping his phone into his pocket, he looked at her with mounting exasperation. 'I don't understand the problem. You work every night in a seedy club. You didn't appear concerned about the social pressures when you were singing to a bunch of strangers.'

'The club is different,' Jessie croaked. 'I'm someone else when I'm there.'

'Well, starting from now, you can learn to be yourself again.' The phone in his pocket buzzed and Silvio retrieved it from his pocket and checked the number. 'I have to take this call. Go and find enough outfits to see you through a month without wearing anything twice. And don't forget beach wear.'

Jessie's mouth fell open and she stared at him but he appeared to have forgotten her existence and she retreated back behind the curtain, carefully removed the dress and put it back on the hanger.

A champagne reception on his yacht?

Deciding that it was better to embarrass herself now rather than later, Jessie stuck her head through the curtain again, her cheeks scarlet. 'I've never been to a party on a yacht. That's basically just a big boat, yes? So I presume I need to wear something practical that will fit under a lifejacket. Trousers or something? Deck shoes?'

He terminated the phone call with a few words of Italian. 'We won't be leaving the marina, so lifejackets hopefully won't be necessary. Definitely no trousers—something glamorous would be appropriate. But I agree that an element of practicality is important. Choose a cocktail dress. Nothing long. And no shoes.'

'No shoes?'

'Heels damage the boat. Go barefoot.'

'What if someone treads on my feet?'

'I'm sure you're used to dealing with awkward customers.'

Jessie caught her breath, wishing she'd never misled him.

Making a decision, she stepped back onto the stage. 'Listen…' She locked her hands together behind her back as if she were standing in the headmaster's study. 'I need to talk to you about my life—'

'I don't want to hear it.' Contempt in his tone, his jaw was clenched hard as he continued to scroll through his emails. 'I can't think of you like that. I can't understand why you would do that.'

'Oh, for goodness' sake!' Jessie marched up the catwalk towards him, forgetting to be self-conscious. 'Switch that wretched thing off and look at me!' She planted herself in front of him. *'Look at me!'*

His gaze locked on hers, his glorious dark eyes shimmering with derision. 'I'm looking.'

And he saw a prostitute, she thought bleakly, her eyes feasting on the bold lines of his face and lingering on his mouth. *The mouth that could drive a woman insane.* Even the scar didn't detract from his monumental sex appeal. If anything, it added to the sense of danger that women found so irresistible.

Even her…

Confused by her feelings, Jessie's courage faltered. 'I—I'm not what you think I am,' she stammered, wishing she'd never misled him in the first place. 'My life hasn't exactly been anything to boast about—I mean, I haven't achieved anything much, but neither have I sunk as low as you seem to think. All I do in Joe's bar is sing.' She said the words fiercely, her gaze fixed somewhere in the middle of his chest. 'Just sing. Nothing else. I sing, I take my money, I go home. Alone.' Every night. Alone. Everything she did, she did alone.

But she wasn't going to think about that now.

She wasn't going to think about how empty her life was. She'd chosen that path, hadn't she?

Her confession fell into a long, tense silence.

'You've paid back twenty thousand pounds,' he drawled, clearly in no hurry to believe her faltering confession. 'Singers at Joe's don't earn that sort of money. Not even with tips.'

'No, they don't, you're right. Which is why I had to find other jobs.' She didn't understand why it suddenly seemed so important that he knew the truth. 'I clean an office block and I work in a café.'

Disbelief shone in his eyes. 'You don't finish work until three in the morning. How can you do two other jobs?'

'I didn't say I wasn't permanently exhausted.' Jessie wrapped her arms around herself, wondering why she'd chosen to say all this standing on a stage. Talk about making a spectacle of herself. Perhaps she should have asked for a megaphone, just to ensure maximum embarrassment. 'There are some days when my feet ache so much I scrub the floors on my hands and knees because it hurts less. And I've been known to drink caffeine nonstop in order to keep myself awake. I admit I'm shattered most of the time. But I'm not what you think I am. And I don't know why you would have thought that. You should know me better.'

He drew in a long breath. 'That dress…'

'It was just a dress, Silvio! It was a bargain. And you're the one who told me that people shouldn't judge each other from the outside.' Exasperated and humiliated, Jessie looked away from him. 'I don't have a lot of money to waste on clothes. Joe likes us to wear something glittery and I saw it in a sale. I thought it looked OK…' Her voice tailed off. 'I know it was revealing but I got more tips that way—have you come so far that you've forgotten how it feels to be desperate for money? And wearing a cheap dress doesn't make a woman a prostitute, Silvio.'

His phone buzzed again but for once he ignored it. 'You told me that you use what God gave you.'

'I was talking about my voice. And I said that after you'd already made your assumption about me.'

There was a long, tense silence broken only by the sound of his breathing and her own heartbeat.

Could he hear it too?

'Why did you let me think that?'

'Why *did* you think it?'

'Because of the place you were singing. The way you looked.' He delivered the words with lethal emphasis. 'The fact that you wouldn't call the police.'

'The police can't handle the workload, you know that. Reporting it to them would have given me more trouble.'

'You needed money. You wouldn't be the first person to choose that route when they're desperate for money.'

'I'm not that sort of woman, you should know that.'

'Should I? I knew you as a girl,' he said softly, his gaze disturbingly acute. 'I don't pretend to know the woman.'

Jessie swallowed, her heart pounding and the blood searing her veins. The heat between them was intolerable and she wondered if he could feel it too or whether the connection was all in her head.

'I'm the same,' she said hoarsely. 'The same person I've always been.'

'No.' His voice was dark, his expression hard as he rose to his feet. 'Everything is different.'

Jessie stood still, transfixed by the hard lines of his profile. He was breathtakingly, spectacularly handsome, and just looking at him drove every thought from her head. *What* was different? What did he mean?

No matter what hovered between them, he was still the man who was responsible for her brother's death. That wasn't going to change.

She was only here because she had no other choice.

'Silvio—'

'The clothes will be sent on,' he said tersely. 'We have a flight to catch and my pilot is waiting.'

CHAPTER FIVE

THE helicopter swooped across the sparkling sea and Jessie gasped because she'd never experienced anything so thrilling in her life before.

'It reminds me of being on a fairground ride.' Breathless, she clutched the edge of her seat, peering out of the window as the turquoise sea flashed beneath them.

'When did you go to a fairground?'

'Johnny took me on my fifth birthday. I remember it clearly.' Through the excitement, she felt the ache build behind her chest. 'I was too small for the roller-coaster so he pushed tissues into my shoes to make me taller.'

Knowing that Silvio would disapprove, she didn't look at him but she could feel him looking at her.

'And did you enjoy yourself?'

'Yes.' Jessie kept her eyes on the water, not confident of her ability to handle this trip down memory lane. 'But Mum was so angry with him. That night of the fair, she'd bought me a really pretty dress and she was afraid I was going to be sick on it. But I wasn't. I have a cast-iron stomach.' The memories were distant—like lights on the shore when you were far out at sea. And they were followed by more painful memories that she didn't want to confront. 'Does it cost a fortune to buy a ticket on this?'

'Why are you asking?'

'Because it's even cooler than your private jet and that was pretty amazing. But even that wasn't as exciting as this. I want to do this again one day.' Distracted by the novelty of the helicopter ride, Jessie lowered her guard. 'One day, when everyone is paying to hear my voice, when I have a major recording contract, I'm going to buy myself a helicopter like this one.'

'You're enjoying yourself that much?'

Jessie turned her head and the intensity of his gaze made her aware of just how much she'd revealed about herself. *She shouldn't be sharing her thoughts with him.*

'I wasn't being serious,' she said lightly, dismissing the confession as unimportant. 'I was only joking. Being silly.'

'There's nothing wrong with dreaming, Jess. Dreams are what drive us forward.'

But there was everything wrong with sharing a dream with a man who had destroyed the most important part of her life.

'So what's your dream?' She seized the opportunity to shift the emphasis of the conversation. 'Why have you returned to Sicily after all these years? I presume it's not a coincidence. Have you rediscovered your roots or something?'

In all the years she'd known him, he'd never mentioned his past. All she knew was the little her brother had told her—that Silvio had spent the first ten years of his life on this Mediterranean island. And that his father had been violent.

'I opened my flagship hotel here recently. It's my biggest project—the culmination of three years of hard work.'

Three years. He'd come to Sicily after her brother had died. *After she'd told him she wanted him out of her life.*

'And that's where the wedding is. But we're going to be staying on your boat, yes?'

'It's a yacht.'

'Same thing.'

'Not exactly,' Silvio said huskily, his eyes dropping to her mouth and lingering there. 'But, yes, we're going to be staying aboard my yacht.'

'So the good thing about a boat—sorry, yacht—is that you can move around. If you're tired of Sicily, you can sail off somewhere else.'

'Exactly.'

Curious, she gave a little shrug. 'So now that you own your own company and you have all that flashy stuff—what is there left to dream about?'

'Life isn't all about possessions, Jess.'

'Easy to say when you have them. What about marriage? Don't you want that?'

'You mean because most men with my wealth should have at least one extremely expensive divorce behind them? I've never felt compelled to go down that route.' Amusement shimmering in his dark eyes, Silvio dragged his gaze from her lips and glanced out of the window. 'We've arrived.'

Why was it that whenever the subject touched on anything personal, he changed the subject? 'How can we have arrived? There's no airport—' Distracted, Jessie looked out of the window and saw a pretty fishing village beneath her. Pastel-coloured houses festooned with flowers followed the curve of the harbour and yachts floated quietly on the clear blue water, their gleaming paintwork sparkling in the bright Mediterranean sunshine. Behind the village she could see mountains and several small churches tucked into the hillside.

A billionaire's playground, Jessie thought wistfully,

looking around for a landing strip of some sort. 'Where are we—?' The question died in her throat as she looked down and saw a landing pad directly beneath them.

'We're landing on a boat,' she said faintly, and heard Silvio sigh.

'Yacht,' he said with exaggerated patience. 'It's a yacht.'

Her head turned slowly and her mouth fell open. 'We're *supposed* to be landing on a yacht? Won't that sink it?' She sensed that he was trying not to smile.

'I sincerely hope not or I'll have nowhere to hold my champagne reception.'

Jessie gaped at him. 'Is that your yacht? But it's huge. When you said a yacht, I presumed you meant something... different.' Something small. She felt as foolish as she'd felt back in his apartment when she'd realised that the room she had been lying in had been his bedroom, not a hotel room.

Feeling out of her depth and insecure, she sat in frozen silence as the helicopter settled onto the deck as lightly as a bird.

A thousand ways to embarrass yourself.

'We're here, Jess.' Apparently oblivious to the range of emotions that held her pinned to the seat, Silvio rose to his feet and held out his hand to her. He was lean, tall, and so obviously out of her league that her stomach lurched.

That was what all the financial generosity had been about.

He hadn't been buying his way out of his guilt.

He'd been trying to turn her into someone he wasn't embarrassed to be seen with.

Ignoring his hand, Jessie picked up her bag and stood up with as much dignity as she could muster. 'Any other surprises for me? Am I going to be wearing the crown jewels with my dress tonight?' Seeing two uniformed crew standing on the deck waiting to greet them, her nerve faltered. 'I'm surprised you didn't fly me in separately so that you don't have to be seen with me.'

'Jessie, relax.'

'Easy for you to say. You're the guy who commutes by helicopter.'

'So do you.' Unperturbed by her sudden attack of panic, he took her hand and drew her towards the steps. 'Don't be self-conscious. No one is judging you.'

'Everyone is judging me,' she muttered, too intimidated to even smile at the crew. 'That's what people do. They're looking at me. They're wondering what you're doing with me.'

'You look fine.'

It was the word he always used. Not sexy, or beautiful or alluring.

Just 'fine'.

She was willing to bet that the women he usually mixed with looked better than 'fine'. It was all too easy to imagine the crew whispering to each other, wondering whether their boss had gone mad.

Jessie glanced down at the beautiful wooden deck and then at the sleek design of the yacht. She didn't fit here, did she? It was all alien to her—he had the super-car, the super-apartment, the super-yacht—the woman he needed on his arm was a supermodel. Not her.

And obviously he knew that, which was why he'd bought her the clothes.

He must be seriously regretting whatever impulse had driven him to rescue her.

He was probably worrying about what hideous faux pas she was going to commit at the champagne reception.

So was she...

Jessie lifted her chin, but nerves fluttered around her stomach. What if no one talked to her? Or maybe, if people thought she was his woman, they'd be scrambling to talk to her just to get close to him. And that scenario would come with its own problems because she had no idea what she was supposed to say about their relationship. They hadn't concocted a story, had they? Where were they supposed to have met? Who exactly was she supposed to be?

Presumably not a penniless nightclub singer in hiding from an unsavoury group of men who wanted to kill her. Imagining the response to that conversation over the canapés, Jessie realised that she didn't have any small talk. What did women talk about at these events? Shoes? Lipstick?

Her lipstick came from the supermarket and she didn't think it would make for an interesting exchange.

Feeling sicker and sicker, she dragged her hand from his grip and stopped walking. 'Wait a moment. Silvio, about tonight—'

'Stop worrying about tonight. Just be yourself.' Clearly unwilling to dwell on the topic, he urged her away from the helicopter and across the deck towards a flight of steps.

Jessie stared at his profile with exasperation.

Be herself?

Surely that was the last thing he wanted.

Being herself would be the equivalent of committing social suicide.

To stand any chance of surviving a champagne reception on board a super-yacht, she had to be someone else.

Someone confident, poised and most of all glamorous.

Someone who could realistically be seen with a man of Silvio's wealth and status.

Jessie's anxiety trebled as she took in the unparalleled luxury and understated elegance of her surroundings. The more she saw, the more intimidated she felt.

She didn't fit in here and she never would.

And then she remembered her wardrobe full of new clothes. Expensive, stylish clothes, all worthy of the woman he wanted her to be.

Couldn't she be that woman?

Frowning slightly, she promised herself that she was going to transform herself and give him a shock.

Tonight, when she dressed for the champagne reception, she wasn't going to be Jessie from the back streets, or Jessie with the gold dress. She was going to dress like someone who dated a billionaire, and when she walked out on the upper deck—or whatever they called the bit of the yacht she was currently standing on—she was going to get more than a 'fine' from him.

As darkness fell and the yacht was illuminated by tiny lights, Silvio greeted the first of his guests. Conscious that there was no sign of Jessie, he glanced around impatiently, his tension mounting with each passing minute.

One glance at her frozen features as she'd stepped from the helicopter onto the deck had been enough to remind him that the tension between them hadn't gone away. She still blamed him for what had happened to her brother and it was obvious that she found the chemistry between them as inconvenient and disturbing as he did.

Silvio gave a cynical smile.

It was clear that had she not been in mortal danger, she never would have accepted his help.

The past stood between them like a solid brick wall.

His mouth tightened. And that was a good thing, wasn't it?

It prevented them from doing something that both of them would regret.

More guests arrived and there was still no sign of Jessie.

Had she decided that she was far enough away from home to take her chances on her own? His brows met in a frown as he considered that possibility but he dismissed it almost instantly. His security team were the most highly trained in the business and, besides, Jessie had been too shaken up by her encounter with those animals to risk leaving.

Exchanging small talk with a famous actress who flirted outrageously, Silvio glanced discreetly at his watch.

In all probability, there was no crisis. She was probably standing in front of the mirror, changing outfits a hundred times.

Five more minutes, and then he was going to look for her.

He was about to extract himself from the actress when she broke off in mid-sentence, a dangerous gleam in her eye as she stared at someone behind him.

'Well—aren't you going to introduce us, Silvio?'

Knowing that sudden chill in her tone could only have been caused by the arrival of an *extremely* beautiful woman, Silvio turned, intrigued as to who could have triggered such a response.

The woman in question stood watching him, the enticing curve of her lips the same shade of vivid red as her sexy strapless dress.

The blood left his brain and it took him several moments to realise it was Jessie.

Jessie as he'd never seen her before.

Unable to help himself, his eyes lingered on her glossy mouth and then moved slowly down her body until he reached her smooth, bare legs. Her feet were as small and delicate as the rest of her, her toenails painted the same shade of bold red. She reminded him of a delicate rainforest bird that had strayed from her normal habitat. Rare, lush, exotic.

She'd left her hair loose, and the soft curls tumbled around her bare shoulders as carelessly as if she'd just left the bed of some very lucky man.

Silvio's mouth dried and his head was full of thoughts he tried never to think about this woman.

His eyes clashed with hers and raw chemistry exploded between them, singeing the air with a dangerous heat that threatened to burn up everything close by.

'Silvio?' The actress's voice poured honey and acid at the same time. 'Aren't you going to introduce us?'

Doubting that he was capable of speech, Silvio licked his lips. 'This is Jessie…' Somehow he managed to make the introductions, but his brain and body were working on entirely different levels.

Fortunately Jessie appeared unaffected. 'So nice to meet you,' she said calmly, as if meeting the cream of Hollywood was a regular occurrence for her. She seemed completely relaxed and not at all starstruck as she made conversation easily.

Her hand slipped into Silvio's and she smiled up at him. 'We have more guests arriving—should we greet them?'

Her use of the word 'we' announced them as a couple, and her subtle reminder that they were supposed to be playing a role penetrated the red mist in Silvio's brain.

He was wishing yet again that he'd thought of a different way to secure her safety when she stood on tiptoe and kissed him lightly on the mouth. Such brief contact shouldn't have had the effect it did, but her sweet lips and the sultry hit of her perfume wrapped around his senses like a magic spell.

Gripped by a raw, primitive hunger, Silvio was forced to confront an inescapable truth—that if it hadn't been for the presence of guests, he would have taken her there and then, against the rail of his yacht, without even bothering to remove the fiery red dress.

Shaken up by the knowledge that he was out of control

for the first time in his life, Silvio took an instinctive step backwards, not trusting himself not to embarrass them both.

What was he playing at?

Fortunately for him an important guest chose that moment to arrive at the foot of the gangplank, and Silvio seized on the opportunity to give himself some much-needed space.

'I'll leave the two of you to get better acquainted,' he said smoothly, extracting himself with almost indecent haste. 'I'll see you later, Jessie.'

He'd left her.

Jessie stood frozen to the spot, scarlet with mortification at his public rejection. Her stomach churning, she stared after his retreating shoulders in disbelief. He hadn't cared whether she was in or out of her comfort zone. He'd just walked away and left her, surrounded by people she didn't know in an atmosphere that was alien to her.

Was she really that embarrassing? He'd stared at every inch of her so it was hard to know which bit she'd got wrong.

She'd tried her hardest to fit in and he'd given her no help at all. Right now she couldn't have felt more out of her depth if he'd thrown her in the water without a life belt.

What was she supposed to do next?

Jessie tried to control her breathing. Her heart was racing, her palms were clammy and she felt the humiliating sting of tears in her eyes. Deciding that holding a drink would at least give her something to do with her hands, she followed the example of the woman next to her and helped herself to a glass of champagne. Were you supposed to hold the stem or the glass? Convinced that everyone was staring at her, she took several mouthfuls and almost choked as the bubbles stung her throat and shot up her nose.

Oh, God, she couldn't even drink champagne without

making a fool of herself. And she should have known better than to touch alcohol. One glass made her talk too much and two sent her to sleep. Either of those scenarios would prove embarrassing and it was obvious that Silvio was already embarrassed enough.

Why?

Was it the dress? She'd tried on what felt like a hundred different dresses before deciding on the red one and she'd been sure that she looked good. So sure, that she'd left her room in a state of excitement, confident that she was suitably dressed for the occasion.

All right, so she'd never actually been on a super-yacht before—or any yacht, for that matter—but the dress was gorgeous and the moment she'd put it on, she'd felt incredible. So incredible that she'd almost danced onto the upper deck, just dying for him to see her—longing to see his reaction.

Only his reaction had been unexpected.

Remembering the expression on his face, the last of Jessie's confidence drained out of her. Given that he was now standing on the other side of the boat, as far away from her as possible, it was fair to assume that the dress was a mistake. Or maybe it was her hair. Or maybe it was the kiss…

He'd actually backed away from her.

And yet this whole thing had been his idea, hadn't it? *He* was the one who had laid down the rules.

Watching the bubbles rise in the champagne flute, Jessie felt a flicker of anger spark under the embarrassment. If he was changing the rules then he could at least have told her.

How could he do this to her?

How were they supposed to convince people that they were together when he was treating her as if she was carrying a contagious disease? Jessie peeped casually through the growing crowd of beautiful people and saw that he had his back to her.

'If you're going to get that upset if he ignores you then you're with the wrong man,' her companion said in a bored tone. 'Silvio is notorious for treating women badly, not that it makes any difference—we still come back for more, don't we? He's so damn handsome, it shouldn't be allowed.'

Did he treat women badly? Jessie suddenly realised that she knew very little about that side of his life except that he was 'choosy'. 'Did you—? Were the two of you—?' She almost choked on the words. 'I mean—'

'Were we lovers?' The woman sipped her champagne, her gaze fastened on Silvio's broad back with almost predatory focus. 'No, not yet. Let's just say it's a work in progress as far as I'm concerned. Me and most of the female population.'

Jessie felt slightly sick. 'If he treats women so badly, I'm surprised you want him,' she said flatly. 'There are plenty of other guys on this yacht—civilised guys who wouldn't treat you badly. Why don't you pick one of those instead?'

'I don't want a nice, civilised guy.' The woman slid a manicured finger around the rim of her glass. 'I want a real man. That's why we women often have affairs with builders and workmen with rough accents and bulging muscles. The irresistible thing about sexy Silvio, apart from the fact he's shockingly handsome and apparently knows exactly how to satisfy a woman in bed, is that he manages to be both rough and tough and a billionaire at the same time.' She sighed wistfully. 'He's a unique package.'

It took Jessie a moment to throw off the disturbing image of a naked Silvio satisfying a beautiful woman in his bed. 'His scar doesn't bother you?'

The woman smiled. 'Let me put this another way. If I'm burgled tonight, I don't want the man I'm with to be locking himself in the panic room until the police arrive. I want a man who is going to protect me.'

Her thoughts full of a dark alleyway and six men in full retreat, Jessie swallowed. 'And you think that's Silvio?'

'Oh, yes….' Her companion took another sip of champagne, but her gaze didn't move from Silvio's back. 'I admit that the thought of all that hard muscle in bed with me is too much to resist. Sorry. But you know what they say. All's fair in love and war.' She lifted her empty glass in a mock gesture of apology and Jessie knew her cheeks were burning.

This woman clearly didn't think she was capable of keeping a man like Silvio and the fact that she was so blatant about it was incredibly upsetting.

Unable to think of a suitable put-down, Jessie stood in frosty silence, wondering how long she was expected to stand there and be humiliated.

The woman helped herself to another glass of champagne from the tray. 'This is absolutely my last glass. Don't let me drink another because the paparazzi have lenses trained on this boat. I have to ask you something—who did your boob job? Did Silvio pay for it?'

'This is my natural shape,' Jessie said through gritted teeth, and the woman smiled.

'Oh, yes, of course it is. Well, pass on my compliments to whoever created your "natural shape". Good luck with Silvio. Enjoy his attention while it lasts.' Without giving Jessie a chance to reply, she strolled off towards a group of women who were laughing close by.

Left standing on her own, Jessie thought she'd never felt more conspicuous in her life. It was better to be part of an uncomfortable conversation than no conversation at all. Aware that everyone was casting curious glances in her direction, she took another mouthful of champagne, more for something to do than anything else. What she really wanted was a large glass of water, but she didn't dare ask—she could see the poor staff were rushed off their feet tending to everyone's whims.

Even though she was standing in a crowd, Jessie felt more isolated and alone than she'd ever felt in her life before.

She didn't fit in here.

Shrinking inside, she felt as though she was on public display, an item of mockery. Small, insignificant and somehow less than these people. When she noticed two women staring at her openly, it was the final straw.

Weaving her way through the glittering, expensively dressed guests, Jessie kept her eyes forwards and walked casually down the steps that led from the upper deck to the sumptuous main deck with its luxurious sofas and glass windows. Ignoring the people gathered there, she just kept on walking, taking another flight of steps that led down to the galley.

Hearing the clatter of pans and the nonstop hum of normal conversation, she gave a sigh of relief and pushed open the door. It was equipped like the kitchens in professional restaurants, the staff clearly prepared to produce anything from a snack to a feast.

The conversation stopped and all the uniformed staff stared at her.

Jessie's friendly smile faltered. 'I—wondered if I could have a glass of water,' she said hesitantly, and a girl with bleached blonde hair hurried to the fridge and pulled out a bottle of mineral water.

'Tap water is fine,' Jessie muttered, but the girl poured the water into a glass and handed it to her.

'You could have asked any of the staff above deck, madam,' the head chef said respectfully, and Jessie blushed, realising that she'd committed another faux pas by walking into the galley.

She didn't fit here either.

'They were busy. I didn't want to bother them. And, anyway, no one up there drinks water. I wasn't even sure you'd have any.' She drank the water. 'And please don't call me madam. My name is Jessie.'

'I'm Stacey.' The young girl who had handed her the water gave her a friendly grin. 'That's a gorgeous dress. Really wicked colour.'

'Do you think so?' Jessie glanced down at herself with a doubtful smile, wishing it had had a similar effect on Silvio.

'It's stunning. I wish I could—'

'Stacey!' The chef's sharp tone silenced the girl and Jessie glanced between them anxiously.

'Look.' She shrugged awkwardly. 'I'm sorry. I probably shouldn't have just barged in like this, but—you're obviously really busy down here. I wondered if I could do anything to help.'

The chef stared at her in stunned silence.

When he didn't answer, Jessie swallowed and gave a faltering smile. 'Obviously not. It doesn't matter, it was only a thought…' She wanted to beg them to let her stay down here with them, but pride wouldn't let her.

'You could wash those champagne glasses,' Stacey blurted out, sending a nervous glance towards the chef. 'Freddie just dropped a whole boxful so we're short.'

The chef looked as though he was about to pass out. 'Stacey—'

'Well, she did ask,' the girl said defensively, and Jessie immediately grabbed an apron from the hook behind the door and tied it round her waist.

'I'd love to wash them.' Without giving the chef time to argue, Jessie hurried over to the sink.

'Madam—'

'It's Jessie.' She started plunging champagne glasses into the hot, sudsy water, the familiarity of the task soothing her. Curves of red lipstick mocked her from the rims of the glasses and she wondered which beautiful woman Silvio was raising a glass with at that moment.

A few minutes later she became aware that the hum of conversation was increasing and soon the kitchen was back to the noisy, bustling workplace it had been a few minutes earlier. Shouts, orders from the chef, and the air filled with the tantalising smell of hot canapés being pulled from the oven. It was a busy working galley with hungry mouths to feed.

After a while, everyone ceased to notice her and the knowledge that none of the other guests were likely to venture down here helped her relax. Jessie continued to wash glasses, listening to the conversation around her even though she was too shy to contribute. As soon as she finished washing one lot of glasses, another set arrived. Gradually she felt the knot of tension in her stomach ease. The ache in her shoulders abated, the sick feeling in her stomach lessened and her heart rate was almost normal.

It was only when a deathly hush fell over the kitchen that she bothered lifting her head to look.

Silvio stood there, a look of stunned incredulity on his handsome face.

He really was the most gorgeous guy she'd ever seen, Jessie thought weakly, feeling the strength ooze out of her limbs.

Even dressed in a dinner jacket, there was a hard, danger-ous edge to him that set him apart from others. On the upper deck she'd spotted no end of good-looking men, but none of them had come close to challenging Silvio for sheer masculine impact. His dark hair gleamed under the harsh lights of the kitchen and his broad, powerful shoulders almost filled the doorway.

'Jessie—?' He seemed to struggle to speak, and Jessie withdrew her hands from the soapy water and stared back at him defiantly, determined to ignore the stab of awareness low in her pelvis, in no hurry to forgive him for leaving her to cope alone among his high-profile guests.

Then she saw the perspiration on the chef's forehead—*perspiration that had nothing to do with the heat of the kitchen*—and decided that it wasn't fair to pull innocent bystanders into the confrontation that was looming.

Taking her time, she dried her hands and removed the apron. 'I've finished the glasses for now. When the next lot comes, just pile them on the side and I'll do them in a minute. Thanks, guys.' Smiling at a white-faced Stacey, Jessie strolled over to the door and stared up at Silvio. 'Have you run out of something up there? Do you need more champagne? Canapés?'

He didn't respond, the gleam in his eyes a warning of his dangerous mood. She sensed he was having trouble controlling his anger, and Jessie wondered why he was angry when *she* was the one who had been cast adrift in a crowd of glittering, intimidating strangers.

'Come with me,' he ordered, and something about his silky-smooth tone made her shiver.

Was she supposed to just follow like an obedient dog?

Tempted to turn back to the washing-up, Jessie looked at the rigid set of his shoulders as he walked out of the door and realised that if she didn't follow him then he'd probably come back and drag her. And she'd had enough public humiliation for one evening.

Glaring at his back, she muttered an apology to the chef and followed Silvio into the stateroom where she'd changed earlier. She closed the door behind her but kept her fingers on the handle. *Ready to escape.* 'What's the matter? Did one of your important guests not show up?'

He turned to look at her, a thunderous expression on his face. 'Do you realise that my entire security team have been looking for you? We were about to involve the local police in the search.'

Stunned by his aggressive tone and the revelation that people had been looking for her, Jessie stared at him blankly. 'Looking for me? Why?'

'Why? Because you went missing,' he said thickly, his voice unsteady and his eyes shadowed. 'No one could find you.'

'I wasn't missing. If they couldn't find me then it's because they weren't looking in the right places.' Acutely aware of the huge bed in the centre of the room, Jessie wished he'd chosen somewhere less intimate for this confrontation. Suddenly she couldn't get the woman's words out of her head—*he knows exactly how to satisfy a woman in bed.*

His gaze held hers with the lethal accuracy of a laser-guided missile and he undid the top button of his shirt with shaking fingers as if he was finding the atmosphere as oppressive as she was. 'It didn't occur to anyone that you'd be in the galley.'

Jessie angled her body so that she couldn't see the bed. 'I wanted a drink of water.' Her explanation drew a glance of blatant incomprehension.

'You don't have to run the tap yourself! If you wanted water, you could have asked one of the staff—'

'No, actually, I couldn't.' His comment made her feel even more gauche. 'They had enough to do running around after your demanding friends.'

Did he even realise that he was standing as far away from her as the room allowed? Was she really that embarrassing? Any further and he'd be standing on the glass-bottomed balcony that was suspended over the water. Her confidence in pieces, Jessie suddenly wished she was back in the alleyway, facing the men who had come looking for her.

At least then she'd known how she was supposed to behave.

'So you thought you'd help them wash up? You're not working in the café now, Jessie. You can do more than that!'

'There's nothing wrong with working in a café. At least in the café people are friendly. They talk to you and they don't look down their noses at you.' Hurt by his obvious desire to keep her at a distance, her insecurities exploded to the surface. 'At the café I know what I'm supposed to be doing!'

'You weren't supposed to be doing anything,' Silvio said harshly. 'I have a large team of staff employed to crew this yacht. All you had to do was enjoy yourself.'

'Enjoy myself? How could I enjoy myself when everyone was staring at me? How do you think I felt up there at your champagne reception, Silvio?'

He lifted his shoulders in an exasperated shrug, as if the answer was obvious. 'Excited? Privileged?'

'Privileged? Where's the privilege in being publicly humiliated?' This time it was her voice that was unsteady and her hand tightened on the door handle, holding it like a lifeline. 'You brought me here, you made me attend an event where you knew I'd stick out and then you just left me! Th-this whole thing was a really stupid idea and I never should have said yes because it was obvious from the beginning that it was never going to work. I don't fit in here and buying me a posh dress isn't going to change that.' She was shaking with anger and she watched his face change as it finally dawned on him that he wasn't handling this well.

'What makes you think you don't fit?' His tone was suddenly cautious and he stared at her the way a parent stared at a child who was on the verge of a major tantrum. 'Did someone say something to you?'

'No—no one said anything, that's the point! They all just ignored me and I stood on my own knowing that they were all talking about me and wondering what I was doing there. I felt like an exhibit in the zoo. They stared so hard I could have charged them for tickets.' Her body was shaking and Jessie fought for control, not wanting him to witness just how bad she felt. 'That's why I went to hide in the galley—I couldn't bear being stared at any longer.'

He drew in a long breath. 'You're being over-sensitive—'

'I am not over-sensitive! Everyone was staring at me and I don't even blame them because they probably took their lead from you. You're so ashamed to be seen with me that you put as much space between us as possible.'

Silvio stilled, a stunned expression on his handsome face. 'You think I'm ashamed to be seen with you? Why would you think that?'

'Apart from the fact that you're standing at the far end of the room right now? Well, let's see…' Jessie tilted her head to one side, her tone sarcastic. 'Possibly something to do with the look on your face when you first saw me, or maybe the fact that you jumped a mile when I kissed you because that's what I thought we were supposed to be doing, or possibly the fact that you ran for cover to the opposite side of the boat, putting as much distance as possible between us. I'm not stupid, Silvio. I know you find me embarrassing.'

'You don't know anything—'

'And you don't have to think up excuses because I know it's all my fault.' She interrupted him before he could say something to make it worse. 'I never should have agreed to this. I'm just a really normal girl who does really ordinary jobs and dressing me up in fancy clothes doesn't change that. I should have known it would never work from the way you reacted when we were in that shop this morning. You couldn't bear to look at me. I am who I am, Silvio, and putting a posh dress on me doesn't change that.'

The sudden flare in his eyes was a reminder of his volatile temperament. 'I am not trying to change who you are.'

'Then why am I dressed like this?'

'Because I thought the clothes would make you feel more comfortable!'

'You mean you didn't want to risk being seen with me when I was wearing my tight gold dress. It's just a shame I seem to embarrass you no matter what I'm wearing.'

Jaw set, mouth hard, Silvio stared at her from the other side of the room. 'Let's get one thing straight. At no point have you ever embarrassed me. That isn't what's going on here.' Even standing still he exuded raw male virility and something about the way he was looking at her made her heart thud uncomfortably against her chest.

'Then what is going on? Up there on the deck you were making a point of not looking at me! You had your back to me, Silvio—you—'

'*Maledezione*, why do you think I had my back to you?'

'Because you're embarrassed that—'

'Don't give me "embarrassed". *Don't* use that word again,' he warned in a driven tone, his voice unsteady and his fingers curled into a fist by his side. There was no evidence of his usual cool control. Instead he looked as though he was on the edge. 'Does no other explanation present itself?' Aggravated to the point of explosion, he simmered like a nuclear reactor on the brink of meltdown. 'You are surely not that naïve, *tesoro*. You know what there is between us. You know what it is that I'm fighting.'

Did she?

Jessie's heart was thundering like a drum roll building up to some startling climax. 'You hate the fact you're attracted to someone like me…?'

'Someone like you?' His tongue barely made it around the words before he finally lost control and blasted her in Italian. Before she could point out that she didn't have a clue what he was talking about, he was across the room. 'Why do you put yourself down all the time? Why do you do that to yourself?' His eyes were narrowed to slits and he planted his arms either side of her, trapping her against the door. 'The reason I stay away from you is not because you embarrass me, or because you don't fit some preordained stereotype, as you seem to think, it's because I've never allowed myself to think of you like that. But I've discovered I'm not as strong as I thought I was.'

'Silvio—'

'Where you're concerned, I'm not strong.' His mouth brushed against hers—a subtle warning, like a predator testing the scent of his prey before devouring it. 'And I can't stay away from you any longer.'

CHAPTER SIX

JESSIE was mesmerised by the hot blaze of sexual intent in his eyes—*by the tantalising brush of his sensual mouth against hers.*

Her stomach curled in delicious awareness and her excitement level rocketed skywards, making her quiver with anticipation as his hard body flattened her to the wall. His muscles were pumped up and hard, his jaw shadowed by stubble, his open shirt showing a hint of bronzed skin and dark body hair. He was irrevocably, unapologetically male and Jessie was completely transfixed by him, so shockingly aroused that she felt as though she was burning alive. The shocking thrill of sexual chemistry arced through her body. When he took her mouth in a hot, demanding kiss she moaned at the erotic slide of his tongue taking the last of the strength from her knees.

Her insides swooped. It was like being back on the helicopter—her senses tumbling over one another, caught in a vortex of excitement so intense that it was almost unbearable.

His hands sank into her hair, his grip almost painful as he held her fast and kissed her as she'd never been kissed before.

And Jessie kissed him back, her response to the explosive chemistry every bit as fierce as his. Her fingers clutched the front of his shirt, her knuckles grazing the hard muscle of his chest, her thighs pressed hard against his.

When he lifted his head, she opened her eyes in shock and tried to focus, only to feel the warmth of his breath on her throat.

'You think you embarrass me, *tesoro*?' He growled the words against her skin, his hands sliding confidently down her back to the base of her spine. 'Do you have any idea how much self-control it has taken not to do this before now?'

Her eyes had closed again and she was panting for air.

With a soft moan, Jessie tore at his shirt and his hands covered hers, completing the task with ruthless efficiency as his mouth found hers again. His kiss was urgent and demanding and she answered that demand with her own. She slid her arms around his neck and rose on her toes to try and get closer, dimly aware that her dress was now in a heap on the floor and she was wearing nothing but a tiny pair of panties. And she didn't even care. She just wanted this wild, delicious excitement to continue for ever.

Without taking his mouth from hers, Silvio scooped her up swiftly and carried her across to the enormous bed. Still kissing her, he deposited her on the centre of the satin cover and came down over her, the weight of his powerful body sending her pulse rate flying.

The pace of it took her breath away and suddenly he reminded her of his Ferrari—super-charged, super-powered, in a different league from others.

Somehow he'd managed to dim the lights in the room and a soft glow came from the illuminated glass balcony and the full moon. Through the open doors she could hear the soothing sound of the sea lapping against the yacht and in the distance the sound of music and laughter. Here, in the intimacy of the master's cabin, it was just the two of them.

Nothing but breathing and heartbeats as he kissed her with relentless expertise. And he gave her no time to think, reason or falter.

When his hand covered the swell of her breast, she gasped, and as his fingers gently teased the soft peak the gasp turned to a moan. And when he dragged his lips from hers and took her nipple into his mouth it was as if someone had plunged a burning sword from her neck to her pelvis and she curled her fingers into the silk sheets and arched her body against his.

Governed by the sensations he'd unleashed in her body, her only focus was relieving the intolerable ache that was building low in her abdomen.

Stunned, shaken and transported to a different world, Jessie was one step behind him all the way so that when she felt him slide down her body and spread her thighs with determined hands, she was unable to do anything except comply.

She felt his strong fingers snap the delicate fabric protecting her, his warm breath tantalisingly close. And then there was only the unerring accuracy of his tongue and each skilled stroke was so maddeningly good that Jessie almost exploded. She shifted and struggled against the silk sheets, desperate to relieve the almost agonising ache, but he gripped her thighs hard, holding her where he wanted her as he continued his erotic feast.

It was too much. Too intense, too shockingly good, and Jessie sobbed his name in desperation as the sensations in her body rocketed skywards. And then he was above her again, and he slid his hand under her bottom and lifted her against him.

'Look at me.' His husky command penetrated the sensual fog that surrounded her brain and her eyes flew to his.

His eyes were fierce, the scar a vivid reminder that this man wasn't the gentle, civilised sort who would buy you dinner and then drop you safely at your door.

And for a single second she was afraid.

'Silvio—'

Still holding her gaze, he lowered his mouth gently to hers, his kiss every bit as explicit and intimate as before, but slower, more measured.

Jessie just had time to reassure herself that he wasn't scary with her when his gaze darkened and he slid his hand under *her* thigh, coaxing her with subtle pressure to wind her leg over his back. She felt the silken heat of him scorch the very centre of her and then he was inside her and it was such an incredible feeling that she cried out his name and dug her fingers into the sleek muscle of his shoulders. He was all raw power and male dominance, his breathing ragged as he thrust deeper still, the primal rhythm joining them completely. Jessie felt a flash of pain so sharp that for a moment she couldn't breathe or move.

Her body tensed and he must have sensed her discomfort because he stilled above her, his breathing harsh as he struggled for control. Visibly challenged by the effort required to hold back, his jaw was tense and his eyes locked on hers.

'Jessie?' He spoke her name through gritted teeth, the muscles in his shoulders rippling as he supported his weight. 'Talk to me…'

But she wasn't capable of speech, shocked into silence by the unexpected pain and unfamiliar intimacy. Then she became aware that he was withdrawing and she slid her hands around his back and arched her hips to stop him. 'No.' She forced herself to relax, rejecting her body's instinct to fight against the strength of his masculine invasion and immediately the pain was replaced by white-hot sexual excitement. She'd never been more aware of the differences between them than she was now—*never more aware of how strong he was and how fragile she was by comparison.*

His hand cupped her face, his gaze irresistibly compelling as he surged into her again, his mouth hovering above hers but not quite touching. They breathed the same air, shared their thoughts through a look rather than words, each oblivious to everything except the other.

Her heart hammered against her chest and she was lost in the delicious world he'd created, a world where there was just the two of them, a world where he protected her and kept her safe—a world of unadulterated pleasure.

Each skilled thrust of his body intensified the excitement, delaying the pleasure until Jessie thought she'd go crazy. Her body fluttered against the length of him and he gave a groan and slowed his rhythm slightly, prolonging the agony for both of them. But she'd been given a brief glimpse of paradise and suddenly she couldn't wait any longer.

Lifting her head slightly, she bit his lower lip and he gave a wicked smile and surged deeper, his mouth taking hers in a hard, demanding kiss. Jessie spun higher and higher, overwhelmed and out of control, until the sensual bonds that had been holding her back snapped and she flew free. She felt herself tighten around him, heard him mutter something in Italian as he powered into her and she felt the hot liquid force of his own release.

It was scorching, intense and utterly consuming, the pulsating pleasure holding them both captive until finally he murmured something in Italian against her neck and rolled onto his back, taking her with him.

He tugged at the silk bedspread and covered them both, even though the evening was warm.

Dazed and shaken, Jessie wondered why he'd done that and then realised that she was shivering.

His strong hand stroked her back gently, warming her, calming her, and she wondered if he'd guessed that her trembling had nothing to do with the temperature of the room.

Now that the wild, crazy storm had passed and her mind had cleared, she was faced with the stark truth.

She hadn't just spent a wild, erotic interlude with an impossibly sexy man.

She'd slept with her enemy.

Silvio looked at the woman lying in his arms and knew she wasn't asleep. She was too still for that.

Never one to avoid a difficult situation, he gave a frustrated sigh and shifted onto his side so that he was facing her. 'Jessie?'

Her eyes remained closed and his mouth tightened. 'You used to do this when you were young,' he muttered. 'You kept your eyes closed whenever something you didn't like was happening.' Her hair was covering part of her face and he moved it with his hand, the scent and the silky softness disturbing his concentration. And he knew his touch affected her too, because there was an almost imperceptible change in her breathing.

'You're going to talk to me eventually, Jess,' he said evenly, stroking her cheek with the back of his fingers, 'so it might as well be now.'

'What do you want to talk about?' She turned and stared straight at him, her green eyes revealing nothing. It was like looking down into the deepest part of the ocean—the surface of the water was just a gateway, concealing a private world beneath. 'Most men want to sleep after sex, not have a conversation. Why do you have to be different?'

'How would you know what men want?' His voice rough, Silvio cupped her face in his hand. Her skin was smooth and soft and he felt a pang of guilt and regret. 'I hurt you, didn't I?' He sensed her immediate withdrawal and instantly regretted both his rough tone and the directness of his question.

'No.' Her eyes were blank of expression. 'You didn't hurt me.' There was no emotion in her tone and Silvio felt a surge of frustration and a flicker of concern.

Suddenly he wished he could read her mind.

'Don't lie to me, Jess, and don't block me out. I want honesty.'

'Do you? All right—I'll be honest.' She pulled away from him and sat up, her tangled hair falling over one shoulder, her gaze fixed straight ahead rather than on him. 'I regret every minute of what we just did. And I hate myself almost as much as I hate you.'

Still shaken by the knowledge that she hadn't slept with a man before and unaccustomed to finding himself in situations where he had no idea how to react, Silvio ignored the part of his brain that was telling him to haul her back into his arms. 'I can understand why you blame me, but—'

'I don't blame you. It was as much my fault as yours. I'm not a child, Silvio. I take responsibility for what I do.' As if she couldn't bear being close to him any more, she slid off the bed and reached for her red dress, every delicious curve visible in the moonlight as she stretched and wriggled back into the crimson tube.

It was like watching an erotic floor show and within seconds he was hard again. It took all his willpower not to drag her back onto the bed, roll her underneath him and repeat the 'mistake' until both of them were too exhausted to analyse anything.

'Why are you getting dressed? It's the middle of the night and the guests went home hours ago.'

'This is the master suite.' Her voice was steady but she

didn't look at him, her hair tumbling over her face as she dipped her head. 'You sleep here. I'll sleep somewhere else. I'm sure this isn't the only bedroom on the yacht.'

In the grip of a volcanic eruption of male hormones, Silvio found it impossible to think clearly. Never before had a woman chosen to leave his bed before he wanted her to, so he had no experience with this type of conversation. 'You sleep where I sleep.'

'No one is watching us now, Silvio. It's just you and me.' She lifted the torn remains of her panties, her face scarlet as she realised they were no longer wearable. Her eyes met his briefly, and Silvio felt the heat sear his flesh because he had an all-too-vivid memory of the moment he'd removed them from her overheated body.

'You're not sleeping in a different bedroom,' he said thickly, his anger with himself turning onto her.

'This charade is over, Silvio. You decided that tonight when you ignored me in public and made love to me in private.'

She was prickly and defensive and nothing like the soft, yielding woman who had responded so passionately.

Was she pushing him away on purpose?

He knew she was hurting badly. And he knew he was the reason. Again.

'I can't imagine what's going through your head right now and I don't pretend to be an expert at reading the female mind,' he breathed, 'so why don't you just tell me?'

'I don't believe in post-mortems, Silvio. If I make a mistake I prefer to move on—leave it behind. It's not a big deal.'

He might even have believed her if he hadn't known her so well. But he saw the pulse beating in her throat and the way her hands shook as she struggled with her zip. The effort required to look indifferent was draining her.

'The first time you have sex should be a big deal.' His voice soft, he watched the colour seep into her cheeks. 'If you'd told me, I would have been gentler with you.' He could have said that if she'd told him, he would have stopped, but he wasn't sure that would have been the truth.

Had he really been capable of that degree of restraint?

She didn't look at him. 'It wasn't the first time I've had sex. Don't be ridiculous.' She yanked impatiently at the zip. 'One minute you think I'm a prostitute, the next you think I'm a virgin—you go from one extreme to the other. And neither is correct. Not that my sex life is any of your business.'

'It's just become my business.'

'Give me a break, Silvio. The one thing I don't need right now is chest-thumping and over-possessiveness. What I do need is air and space. So please don't follow me.' Like a trapped animal making a frantic attempt to escape from captivity, she shot out of the room and Silvio covered his eyes with his forearm and swore long and fluently in Italian.

Her body aching in unfamiliar places and her feelings a tangled mess, Jessie took the first set of steps she saw. And then another set.

She was running. Not just from Silvio but from the intense feeling of guilt that sucked her downwards at a terrifying speed. As the panic spread through her like some deadly disease, she felt as though her brother was watching her, his face twisted into a mask of condemnation.

No, Jessie, not that. Not him.

Sleeping with Silvio felt like the ultimate betrayal.

Gasping for air, she found herself at the prow of the yacht and closed her fingers over the metal rail, fighting for control. Out here in the fresh air, with the sea breeze cooling her skin, she couldn't understand why she'd let it happen.

Why hadn't she just said no?

Lowering her forehead onto her hands, she gave a low groan of despair. Lying to him was one thing, but what was the point of lying to herself? She hadn't said no because she hadn't wanted to say no. She'd dreamed about this moment for as long as she could remember and if it hadn't been for Johnny…

'You're torturing yourself for no reason.' The soft male drawl came from behind her and she lifted her head but didn't look round.

'Go away. I'm not going to jump, if that's what's worrying you.'

'It isn't.' He was silent for a moment. 'Whatever you think, Johnny would have wanted you to be happy.'

Jessie lifted her head and stared into the darkness, listening to the sea and the night-time breeze playing with the mast. The lights from the yacht illuminated the surface of the water and the peace of the night seemed only to emphasise the turbulence inside her. 'I don't want to talk about my brother.'

'You can't go through life avoiding every subject that hurts.'

'All right, let me put this another way.' Her fingers tightened on the rail but she didn't turn. 'I don't want to talk about my brother with *you*.'

'Fine. I'll talk. You listen.' His voice was rough. 'If he were standing here now, he wouldn't be blaming you, he'd be blaming me.'

'Well, he'd be wrong. You're not responsible for my decisions, Silvio. I'm the one who followed you into the bedroom—'

'And I'm the one who crossed the room. I'm the one who finally snapped. It was always going to happen. And Johnny knew it.'

Suddenly it was difficult to breathe. 'That's not true.'

'Why do you think he was always so protective of you?'

'He was my big brother—'

'And he felt the chemistry between us. He knew how I felt about you. And he was scared for you. He thought you were too young to be involved with someone like me and he was right. You were.'

His words were such a shock that they took a moment to sink in and when they did the effect on her was profound.

The knowledge that Silvio had felt that way about her for so long was more intoxicating than the champagne and Jessie felt a dangerous heat spread through her limbs. 'That doesn't make sense.' Her fingers were holding tight to the rail. 'You never looked at me.'

'And you have no idea how much self-discipline that took.'

It was unspeakably painful, hearing the words she'd always dreamed of hearing when it was too late. But, still, she had to know.

'I wasn't a child. You could have said something. I don't believe for a moment that if you really wanted something you would have let my brother stop you.'

'I would have done, but then Johnny chose to put himself between us in the most effective way possible.'

Jessie closed her eyes. 'That's an awful thing to say.'

'He was frightened of losing you, Jess. All his real friends had turned away from him. The only people he saw were dealers and people like him. And you. No matter what squalor he lived in, no matter how low he sank, you were always there for him.'

'He was my brother.' She whispered the words into the darkness. 'I would always have been there for him no matter what he did or who I was with.'

'But his mind was too twisted from the drugs to see that clearly. You were as important to his survival as the syringes and that filthy stuff he craved.'

'If you hated that "filthy stuff" so much, why did you give him the money to buy more?'

'Because I made an error of judgement.'

'And is that what happened tonight? Another error of judgement?' It felt strange, having this conversation in the semi-darkness, without looking at him. But it made it easier somehow. *Easier to say what needed to be said.*

'Tonight wasn't an error of judgement. More a loss of control.' Coming from him that was quite an admission and Jessie gave a tiny laugh.

'Don't blame yourself. I could have said no.'

'Did I give you a chance?' His hands closed over her shoulders, turning her to face him. 'Did I give you time to think or hesitate?'

'I could have stopped you.'

'Because you're so much stronger than me?' He gave a grim smile, his hands exerting minimum pressure as he backed her against the rail, proving his point with ridiculous ease.

'I didn't say you weren't strong.' Her heart was racing in a crazy, dangerous rhythm. 'I said I could have stopped you.'

'How?' The harshness of his tone made her flinch and she wondered if he even realised that his fingers were digging into her flesh.

'I would have asked you,' she said softly. 'And you would have listened.'

And she knew it was true. Yes, he was strong—so much stronger than her that any comparison would have been ridiculous. But she knew he would have stopped if she'd said the word.

His grip on her arms eased. 'I wouldn't be so sure about that.'

He was trying to make her feel better—trying to erase the terrible guilt—but she knew that nothing would do that. She'd carry the betrayal with her for ever.

'We won't mention it again.' Jessie stared at a point in the middle of his chest, afraid that if she met his eyes she'd be lured into the same intoxicating paradise from which she'd just escaped.

'You think that's it?'

'Yes, that's it.' Blanking the expression from her eyes, she looked at him. 'Perhaps you're right, Silvio. Perhaps this thing has been simmering between us for a long time. In which case it's a good thing that we've got it out of the way. We can put it behind us now.'

His hands tightened again. 'That's a very casual response from a woman who has just had her first sexual experience.'

'You're not my first.' Desperate now, she selected the words that she knew would drive him away. 'Which is probably just as well or you would have put me off. Your caveman approach to love-making wouldn't be the best introduction to the pleasures of the bedroom. Generally I prefer more in the way of foreplay.' It was a lie, but she must have sounded convincing because his hands dropped from her shoulders.

'I did hurt you.'

'Yes, you did.' She forced the second lie past her lips, wondering why it felt so hard. She shouldn't care about his feelings, should she? 'Physically we're obviously not that compatible.'

'You're very small—'

'And you're very rough.' Yet another lie. He hadn't been rough. True, he hadn't been as careful with her as he would have been if she'd told him the truth, but that was her fault, wasn't it? 'Probably not a good combination. Still, at least we got it out of our systems.' Jessie turned away, her legs shaking and a sick feeling in her stomach.

It felt wrong to dismiss the incredible intimacy they'd shared with such careless words but it was the only way she knew that might prevent him from touching her again. And it was imperative that he didn't touch her again.

'Go back to the master suite.' He moved to let her past, his tone tightly controlled, his features revealing nothing. 'Take a bath and get some sleep. I'll sleep elsewhere.'

So he'd believed her, then.

She should have felt relief that her words had been so incredibly effective.

Instead, she felt sick. As if she'd destroyed something rare and special.

She'd insulted him in the most personal way possible and his Sicilian pride would never allow him to forgive that.

And that, Jessica thought numbly, was that. A few well-chosen words were all it took to kill off perfect chemistry.

The emotional barrier that had kept them apart had been strengthened and was now an immovable force.

CHAPTER SEVEN

DESPITE the stress, Jessie slept. But sleep gave her little respite because Silvio featured in every one of her dreams. Unfortunately for her mental state, her dreams had exaggerated him back into the shape of a hero.

He was the man who had rescued her from danger in the alleyway. He was the man who had brought her to safety. He was the man who had made sure that any physical relationship she ever had in the future would be an anticlimax…

With a groan she woke up and buried her face in the pillow.

He was also the man who was responsible for the death of her brother.

But suddenly everything that had been clear was confused.

Instead of blaming him, she was thinking about his hands on her body and his mouth on hers. Instead of hate she felt another, more dangerous emotion that she didn't dare examine too closely.

And what was the point of thinking about it when it was over before it had started?

She'd driven him away, hadn't she?

I've wanted you since you were eighteen.

Jessie put her hands over her ears, trying to block his

words from her head. She didn't want to think about what would have happened if he'd told her how he felt years ago. She didn't want to think what might have happened if, instead of keeping his distance, he'd decided to take what he wanted.

She gave a shiver, thinking of what he'd said about everyone deserting Johnny.

He hadn't deserted him, had he?

He'd been there right until the end.

He'd talked about Johnny being self-destructive and it was true.

She'd wanted to save her brother, she'd wanted him to change—but he hadn't been able to. And she'd been angry with him for not trying harder.

Confused, Jessie slid out of bed and opened a cupboard. Removing the shoebox from its hiding place, she lifted the lid and stared down at her life.

The photographs were all she had of her brother.

That and the battered, scruffy stuffed bunny Johnny had given her one birthday.

They were all that remained of her past. That, and the memories.

Underneath the photographs, something shone and she dipped her hand into the box and pulled out the locket.

She hadn't allowed herself to look at it for three years.

Unsettled by her thoughts and desperate for distraction, Jessie dropped the locket back into the box and walked into the luxurious bathroom. But she didn't feel like lying in a bath with her thoughts so instead she took a quick shower and changed into a simple summer dress.

Then she left the owner's suite and walked towards the galley. She had no idea where Silvio had spent the night but after his comments the night before, it was fairly safe to assume that he wasn't going to be anywhere near his own kitchen.

Stacey was there, chopping carrots into tiny batons. When she saw Jessie, she put down the knife and gave a friendly smile.

'Fancy a coffee? I can make you a cappuccino.'

'That would be lovely, thanks.' Jessie settled herself on a stool in the corner of the kitchen and watched as Stacey prepared the coffee and foamed the milk in a jug.

'So what did you do before this? I suppose Silvio kidnapped you from some Michelin-starred restaurant, did he?'

Stacey sprinkled chocolate powder onto the creamy froth. 'Not exactly.' She put the coffee down in front of Jessie and gave a little shrug. 'Actually, I was in a spot of trouble,' she said calmly. 'I was sleeping rough and doing stuff I shouldn't have been doing. If it hadn't been for the boss, I'd still be there. Or worse.'

Jessie poked the foam with a spoon. 'What did he do?'

'He gave me a chance, that's what he did.' Stacey returned to her chopping. 'Same as he does for all the people who work for him.'

'What do you mean?'

'All the people who work for him…' Stacey put a pan on the heat and started frying an onion. 'They nearly all have some sort of past. I suppose it's because he grew up on the streets himself. He knows how easy it is to get into trouble. But I guess you know that. The boss doesn't believe in hiding all that stuff, which is good really, because keeping up an act is exhausting.'

Jessie put the spoon down slowly. 'Are you saying that all the people who work for him have been in trouble? What sort of trouble?'

'Different stuff. Some minor, some major.' Stacey added chopped herbs to the onion and removed the pan from the heat. 'The thing about Silvio is that he's willing to give you a chance if you want one. He believes people can change if they're given a chance. But it's only ever one chance. Mess up and you're out. But mostly people don't. If you're handed a lifeline, you take it, don't you?'

She'd taken it.

Then Jessie thought of her brother. He hadn't taken it, had he? 'Not always. Some people just can't help themselves.' She rubbed her fingers along her forehead, trying to ease the uncomfortable thoughts she was having.

Had she been unfair to Silvio?

Stacey rinsed the knife under the tap. 'Some people are too messed up, I suppose. Or perhaps they just don't want to be saved. But at the end of the day there's only so much someone else can do, isn't there? They can give you a ladder but it's up to you to climb up it.'

Was it that simple? Silvio should have known that Johnny would misuse the money, shouldn't he? He should have known that Johnny didn't have the strength to resist temptation. He wasn't blameless. 'Why does he employ people who have been in trouble—is it cheap labour?'

'You're more cynical than I am and, no, it's not cheap labour. He pays well.' Stacey reached for the olive oil. 'When you come out of prison, it's hard to get a job. Employers just won't take a chance on you. Silvio does. He doesn't care what's in your past.'

'So he's a soft touch.'

'Soft?' Laughing, Stacey finished what she was doing and washed her hands. 'He's about as soft as steel. And clever.'

'But—'

'He gets something back that money can't buy, and that's loyalty. He has virtually zero staff turnover. Not one of his employees has ever sold him out to the press, or anyone else for that matter. They just wouldn't. We all owe him.'

None of that changed the fact that if Silvio hadn't given Johnny the money, her brother might still be alive.

'How many of his staff…?' Jessie felt awkward finishing the question but Stacey just grinned.

'Did he drag from the streets? Dunno. He treats us all the same, you see, so you'd never know. Do you want another coffee?'

'She doesn't have time.' Silvio strode across the galley and took Jessie's hand in his, pulling her off the stool. 'The helicopter is waiting. Stacey, you have five minutes to put together a delicious picnic. Something special.'

'Yes, boss.' Rising to the challenge with a delighted grin, Stacey shot towards the enormous fridge, obviously only too pleased to show what she could do.

Jessie's face was scarlet—partly because she'd been caught talking about him but mostly because seeing him in daylight after what they'd shared the night before felt hideously awkward. Her stomach cramped and her pulse rate doubled. She didn't want to look at him and yet she couldn't *not* look. She wanted to ask him why they needed a picnic when they had nothing more to say to each other, but she felt too self-conscious to speak to him in front of Stacey. His hand still held hers tightly and the warmth and strength in his grip did something strange to her insides.

Wasn't he angry with her?

After what she'd said to him the night before, he should have been angry.

And after her conversation with Stacey, she no longer knew how she felt.

Oblivious to the atmosphere between the two of them, Stacey was moving around the kitchen efficiently, chopping, wrapping, washing salad and adding various items to a large coolbox. Then she winked at Silvio and added a bottle of champagne and some glasses. 'Just in case you're thirsty, boss. Do you want me to have it taken to the helicopter?'

'No, I'll take it myself.' Silvio held out his free hand and gave Stacey a rare smile. *'Grazie.'*

'Prego,' Stacey said in a broad London accent, and Silvio winced.

'You really must work on that accent. Tell Chef we won't be back for dinner tonight.' Without giving Jessie the opportunity to question that command, he tightened his grip on her hand and walked purposefully towards the upper deck.

Wondering whether he'd overheard any of her conversation with Stacey, Jessie tugged at her hand. 'Wait—Silvio—' It felt as though everything was shifting around her and she couldn't keep her balance.

'I'm not good at waiting.' Still pulling her along with him, he didn't slacken his stride and she wondered why it was that he was always so sure of everything he did.

Life wasn't that black and white, was it?

Jessie couldn't stand the tension any longer. She had no idea where they were going or why, but she knew she had things to say. 'At least tell me where we're going.'

'Somewhere we can be together without an audience.' Without pausing, Silvio took the steps that led to the small helicopter pad. 'Somewhere we can talk.'

'What is there to say?' Was he expecting her to apologise for what she'd said to him?

'Plenty.' His eyes unfathomable, Silvio touched her cheek gently with his fingers and then urged her onto the helicopter. He spoke to his pilot in Italian and moments later they were lifting into the air and the yacht was suddenly far beneath them.

'Where are we going? What are we doing?' Jessie turned towards him and he relaxed in his seat.

'Consider it foreplay,' he said huskily, a sardonic smile

tugging at the corners of his mouth as his eyes made contact with hers. 'Generally you like plenty of foreplay—wasn't that what you told me? I'm giving you what you want, *tesoro*.'

How could he possibly know what she wanted when she had no idea herself?

The sudden dive of her stomach had nothing to do with the movement of the helicopter.

'I didn't mean—I was just—'

'I know what you were doing. I know far more than you think I do.' He slipped his hand under her chin and turned her face to his. 'And the pretence ends now.'

'There is no pretence, Silvio, I'm—'

'Relax. If you look below you now you can see Mount Etna,' he interrupted her, ignoring her agitation. 'She is much like a woman. When she's in a bad mood she grumbles and spits fire.'

Desperately aware of him, Jessie dragged her eyes from his and stared down at the flanks of the volcano but even the wild beauty of the landscape couldn't distract her. 'At least tell me where we're going.'

'To a beach that you can only reach from the air' was all he would say, and Jessica gasped when she finally spotted the horseshoe of perfect white sand beneath them.

'That's where we're going? How are we going to land?'

'Safely,' Silvio purred, casting an amused smile towards his pilot, 'or he's fired.'

Jessie gripped the edge of her seat as the grinning pilot lowered the plane onto the sand, his blades dangerously close to the cliffs that gave the beach its privacy. It was a breath-takingly daring piece of flying and she wondered if she was going to end her days in a mangled heap of wreckage.

It was only when Silvio gently uncurled her fingers from

the seat that she realised they'd landed safely. 'Move. He can only stay here for a few seconds.'

Jessie stumbled onto the soft, white sand and he pulled her against him as the helicopter rose into the air and left them alone. As the helicopter became a speck in the distance, Silvio led her to the far side of the beach where the steep cliffs created an oasis of shade. Then he opened a bag that he'd removed from the helicopter, threw a soft blanket onto the sand and handed her a package.

'This is for you.' Without waiting for her response, he stripped off his shirt and dropped it onto the blanket with a characteristic lack of inhibition.

Still clutching the small parcel, Jessie stared dry-mouthed at his bronzed, muscular torso. His stomach was flat, his shoulders wide and his chest shadowed with dark hair that seemed to accentuate his masculinity.

He had an incredible physique and suddenly she remembered what he'd said about foreplay.

Apparently oblivious to her scrutiny, his hand dropped to his zip and Jessie dragged her eyes away from his bronzed abdomen and stared at the sea, trying to ignore the dangerous warmth low in her pelvis.

What was he doing?

After what she'd said to him last night she hadn't expected him to speak to her again. She certainly hadn't expected him to maroon them on the equivalent of a desert island.

'What is this place?' She stared straight forward but her shoulders tensed as she heard the slide of his zip and the tantalising rustle of fabric. 'Where are we?'

'It's my private bolt-hole. Somewhere no one else can join us. We're alone.'

A thrill of excitement shot through her and Jessie shivered as his strong, confident hands curled over her shoulders.

'You need to relax,' he said evenly, massaging her skin slowly. 'You're extremely tense.'

Of course she was tense.

'Silvio, there are things I really have to say to you—'

'You said them last night. Don't forget sunscreen.' Flashing her a disturbingly attractive smile, he passed her a tube and Jessie glared at him in frustration.

'I want to talk!'

'Relax,' he said softly. 'We have all day. We don't have to rush anything. Open the package, Jessie.'

Frustrated with him, her hands shaking, Jessie put down the sun cream and opened the package, staring at the minuscule gold bikini in disbelief. 'You have to be joking. And you thought my dress was indecent...'

His eyes gleamed with undisguised amusement. 'This is going to be a private show. Unless you'd rather be naked. I thought you might be too modest for that, but I could be wrong. After all, you keep telling me how experienced you are and an experienced woman would be confident enough in her body to swim naked, isn't that right? The decision is yours.'

With a seductive smile, he sprinted towards the shoreline and plunged into the sparkling turquoise sea. Watching him swim away from her with a powerful crawl, Jessie tightened her grip on the bikini in her hands.

A private show?

He wanted her to wear it for him. And she felt far too self-conscious, which was completely ridiculous given what they'd shared the night before.

Instead of changing, Jessie sat down on the rug, looped her arms round her knees and waited for him to return, still confused about why he'd brought her here.

Her thoughts were a tangled mess but she had an uncomfortable feeling that she owed him an apology.

He'd been trying to help Johnny—like he was helping all of the others; *like he'd helped her.*

When he finally strolled up the beach towards her, she was rigid with stress and braced for a difficult conversation.

Silvio ran his hand over his face to clear the water, and stooped to retrieve a towel from the rug next to her, supremely comfortable with himself. 'Didn't it fit?'

Realising that she still had the minuscule bikini clamped in her hand, Jessie released it. 'I don't know. I didn't try it on. Silvio, there is something I really need to say to you.' Her lips felt stiff and he gave a sigh, looped the towel around his lean hips and sat down on the rug next to her.

'All right. Let's get the talking part out of the way.' His gaze focused on her face and there was something so mesmerising about his eyes that Jessie suddenly found it difficult to breathe.

'I can't concentrate when you look at me like that.'

'Like what?'

'Like you want to…' Her mouth dried and he gave a slow, dangerous smile.

'I do want to. I think I made that clear last night. But you obviously have things you want to say, so why don't we get that out of the way first?'

First?

Hearing him say he wanted her drove all thoughts from her brain. 'Could you move back a bit?' she blurted out. 'I can't think when you're sitting this close.'

A sardonic smile on his face, he shifted away from her. 'Better?'

'Not really.' Jessie turned her head away, trying to resist the temptation to stare greedily at his bronzed shoulders and powerful chest. No one else had ever had this effect on her before and she had no idea how to deal with it—how to control it. The feeling was too big. Too powerful.

'Jessie…' His voice gentle, he reached out a hand and drew her face round, forcing her to look at him. Trapped by his gaze, she was dimly aware of the sudden changes in her body—the increase in her heartbeat, the melting feeling that started in her throat and spread slowly down all the way to her knees. She knew that if she'd needed to run now, she wouldn't have been able to. Possibly not even walk. It was as if he'd cast an invisible spell over her body, the chemistry holding her captive.

For a moment neither of them spoke. His eyes dropped to her mouth and he leaned forward slightly as if he intended to kiss her. It was the merest hint of movement but it was enough to set off a chain reaction inside her. He hadn't touched her, and yet the mere thought of him triggered the same wild response that had erupted the night before. The world around them ceased to exist and they were trapped inside their own invisible bubble of intimacy.

Jessie held her breath, sensing that she was poised on the brink of another wild, crazy ride and then he said something under his breath in Italian and tore his gaze from hers as if he too was disturbed by the astonishing connection.

'You want to talk about Johnny.'

Dizzy and disorientated, Jessie tried to focus. 'How do you know that?'

'You're easy to read.'

She sincerely hoped she wasn't. If he could see what was going on in her head at that precise moment, she'd be too embarrassed ever to look at him again.

Trying to keep her mind on what she wanted to say, Jessie rubbed the tip of her finger over the blanket, mindlessly tracing the pattern to try and keep her mind on what needed to be said. 'I said some awful things to you about Johnny—

I see now that you thought you were helping.' She'd imagined it would have been easier to look elsewhere, but her eyes were drawn back to his.

'You were right to blame me. I gave him the money.'

'You gave him a chance,' Jessie said huskily, Stacey's words clear in her head. 'And he chose not to take it. You tried to help him. And he rejected that help.'

'Don't make me into some sort of hero, Jess.' His voice rough, Silvio's beautiful mouth curved into a cynical smile. 'I gave him the money because I could. It wasn't a big sacrifice on my part. And I made a gross error of judgement. He told me that he was serious about getting his life together. That this time he was going to come off the drugs. I believed him and I shouldn't have done.'

'Johnny could be very convincing.' Jessie forced herself to confront issues she'd never confronted before. 'I think addicts can be like that. Selfish. Persuasive. Dishonest. They'll go to any lengths to get their fix. He stole from me, you know. I refused to give him cash, so he just took it.' It was something she'd shut from her mind, preferring to remember the good things about her brother.

And bad things about Silvio.

'I know that he stole from you.' Tiny drops of seawater still clung to his bare shoulders, glistening like diamonds in the bright sunlight. 'That's the other reason I gave him the money. I was frustrated seeing you work so hard to keep him.'

'You did it for me…'

'Yes, ironic, isn't it—that it backfired so spectacularly?' His eyes darkened and Jessie's stomach melted, her desperate longing for him so intense that the tips of her fingers tingled with the need to touch him.

But even while her body was reacting, her brain was still holding her back.

She'd been angry with him for so long, it wasn't easy to let it go.

'Time for a swim.' Silvio sprang to his feet in a fluid movement and held out his hand. 'Are you wearing the bikini or swimming naked?' His tone velvety soft and tinged with amusement, he stooped and retrieved the bikini from the rug. 'On second thoughts, I'm not giving you a choice. If you don't want a repeat of last night, you'd better wear something.' His searing glance made her catch her breath and she realised that nothing she'd said to him had altered the chemistry between them.

'I can't swim,' she admitted. 'I never learned. My childhood didn't exactly include lessons at the local pool.'

He pushed the bikini into her hands. 'I'll teach you.' And then he was sprinting across the sand away from her and into the cold water.

This time Jessie didn't hesitate. She changed swiftly, not giving herself time to question her decision. The sand was hot on her bare feet and it was a relief to splash into the clear water. She waded in as far as her knees and then stopped.

Without warning, Silvio scooped her up in his arms and carried her deeper. She clung around his neck, her eyes drawn to the dark shadow of his jaw.

He was so strong.

'If you drop me now,' she warned, 'I'll never forgive you.'

'I'm not going to drop you, but you can't learn to swim in shallow water.'

'I want to be able to touch the bottom.'

'If you can touch the bottom, you'll walk, not swim.' Without releasing his hold on her, he lowered her into the water and she gasped.

'It feels deep.'

'I'm still standing up.'

'But you're taller than me!' She clung to his neck. 'I mean it, Silvio, if you let me go, I'll drown.'

'Do you really think I'd let you drown?' His eyes were fierce as he pulled her hard against him. 'Do you really think I'd let anything happen to you if it was in my power to stop it?'

His body was hard against hers and she couldn't help be aware of the change in him.

'You see?' His voice was full of self-mockery. 'Even cold water doesn't help.' Without giving her time to answer, he shifted her away from him and guided her onto her stomach. 'You're out of your depth because it's easier to learn this way. My hand is underneath you so you're not going to sink. Now kick your legs.'

Jessie wanted to ask him how she was supposed to learn to swim when all she could think about was his hand on her stomach, but she didn't want to admit how much he affected her. Determined to impress him, she kicked her legs and followed his instructions. For the next half an hour she did everything he told her, forcing herself to concentrate on staying afloat in the water, rather than on him.

Her face set with determination, she did what he'd taught her. 'Try letting go of me,' she panted, and Silvio gave a soft laugh.

'I let go of you ten minutes ago, *tesoro*. You've been swimming on your own since then.'

The shock made her stop moving her legs and instantly she sank like a stone, taking a mouthful of water on the way. Strong hands locked around her waist and lifted her and she gasped in the air, coughing and choking.

'Don't try and breathe under the water,' he advised, and Jessie pushed her hair out of her eyes so that she could glare at him properly.

'You should have told me you were letting go.'

'You swam perfectly. It was only when you thought about what you were doing that you sank. You need to have more faith in yourself, Jess.' He pulled her against him and her legs wrapped themselves around his waist.

As always she felt incredibly safe with him and she knew that there was no one else in the world she'd rather cling to in deep water.

The sun burned her shoulders and the salt water stung her eyes but she'd never been happier in her life, and when he pressed his mouth gently to hers the flash of excitement was instantaneous, so intense, that she pressed against him and opened her mouth under his.

'Careful,' he growled against her lips, 'or all the cold water in the world isn't going to help me.'

Surprised by the comment, Jessie pulled away slightly. 'That's why you wanted me in the water?'

He gave a wry smile. 'Let's just say that the self-control on which I pride myself appears to be non-existent where you're concerned.'

Feeling a rush of excitement that she had that degree of effect on him, Jessie slid her hands into his wet hair. 'You're saying I'm irresistible?'

His jaw tightened and she had a feeling he was gritting his teeth. 'Something like that. If you don't want to make it worse for me, you could stop wriggling.'

Jessie stilled, but the urge to move her hips was almost painful. 'We could go back to the beach…'

'No.' His mouth drifted over hers with tantalising slowness. 'Not yet. You wanted foreplay. This is foreplay. If I die in the attempt, you'll have to resuscitate me.'

'Mouth to mouth.'

'You're already doing that part.' His hands were tight on

her hips, although whether he was holding her against him or preventing her from pressing any closer, she wasn't sure. All she knew was that her entire body was on fire.

'I think foreplay might be overrated.'

'Don't be impatient.' His tongue traced her lower lip, teasing, coaxing until Jessie's entire body was burning.

Unable to help herself, she ground her hips against him and he gave a throaty groan and tightened his grip on her thighs.

The contrast of the cool water against her heated skin somehow intensified the whole experience and Jessie moaned with relief as he slid one hand down her back and then lower still.

Tensing with anticipation, the entire focus of her body was centred on that one part of her, and when his skilled, gentle fingers finally touched her there she almost passed out with pleasure.

'Are you sore after last night?' His intimate question increased the colour in her cheeks.

'No.'

'This time I'm not going to hurt you,' he promised thickly, and Jessie gave a low moan of desperation.

'If you don't do something soon, I might have to hurt *you*,' she muttered, and he gave a faint laugh and took her mouth again, his kiss gentle but explicit.

His fingers continued their intimate exploration but it wasn't enough and Jessie shifted against him, too aroused to control her movements.

She felt his other hand on her thigh and then the bottom half of her bikini dropped away and she felt cool water against the burning centre of her body—*felt him hard and ready, against her*.

His mouth still on hers, Silvio anchored her hips and held

her still, his fingers tight on her trembling thighs as he eased into her gently. He felt smooth and hot and she cried out against his mouth and tried to take him deeper but he held her fast, the strength of his hands preventing any movement on her part.

He seemed determined to torture her, his movements so slow and provocative that Jessie felt as though her entire body was going to explode. The contrast between his powerful heat and the coolness of the water made the experience all the more intense and she moaned his name in quiet desperation.

The only sound was the hiss of the water as it touched the beach and the harsh sound of his breathing as he struggled for control.

'Can you feel me?' His voice husky, he drew his mouth from hers just enough to speak. 'You're mine now, Jessie. No one else's.'

She was about to say that she didn't want to be anyone else's but then he finally released his iron grip on her hips and allowed her the freedom she craved. The sinuous movement of her hips took him deeper still and her eyes drifted shut because it was no longer possible to think of anything except how he felt inside her. He was silk and steel, raw passion and elemental energy, but most of all he was her man.

The only man she'd ever wanted.

He drove deep inside her, his rhythm smooth and controlled, so skilled that she might have thought he was detached about it if she hadn't opened her eyes to look at him. One glimpse of his taut features revealed how much it was costing him to hold back and she kissed him hungrily, her tongue seeking his.

'Silvio—please…' she begged against his mouth, driven wild by the electric sensations shooting through her body.

Didn't he feel the same way? Or was he determined to prove that he was capable of control around her?

If that was the case then he obviously lost the battle because he gave a low growl and surged deeper, the movement driving her higher and higher until she was poised on the edge of paradise. Jessie couldn't breathe or think. She was aware of nothing except what his body was doing to hers. And then he drove into her one more time and she was caught in an explosion of ecstasy, the pleasure so sublime that her mind shut down. As her orgasm fluttered along the length of him she heard him groan and lose control, both of them flying upwards to the same place.

As she gradually returned to earth, Jessie dropped her head against his shoulder, breathing in the scent of his damp flesh. 'If you let go of me now,' she whispered, 'I'll definitely drown.'

He didn't answer and a moment later he shifted his grip on her, swung her into his arms as if she weighed nothing and carried her back to the beach.

'I'm not wearing anything,' Jessie muttered against his neck, and his hold on her tightened.

'Get used to it. Apart from public appearances, that's the way you're going to be from now on.'

'Public appearances?' She thought about the night before. 'I just don't feel comfortable with those people, Silvio.'

'That's because last night I left you on your own, but that won't happen again.' He lowered her onto the blanket and shifted himself over her, his eyes holding hers. 'Everything is different now. This isn't for show. This isn't for anyone else. It's for us.'

CHAPTER EIGHT

Was this really her life?

The days that followed were so blissful they felt unreal.

Silvio was extraordinarily attentive, and when he wasn't making love to her he was showing her Sicily, swapping the luxury of his yacht for the luxury of his Maserati as he drove her around the island.

'You have a car in every port,' Jessie said dryly, but she was enchanted by what she saw. Almond groves and vineyards, narrow streets with crumbling houses, honeyed by age. Ancient churches, small children playing in the sunshine and a pace of life so slow it was almost standing still.

Absorbing everything around her, Jessie realised that she'd rarely thought beyond her own little world. Places like this hadn't existed for her, except in the windows of travel agents.

But this was Silvio's life. He'd travelled all over the world.

The wind whipped her hair across her face and Jessie anchored it with her hand, telling herself that it didn't matter that she hadn't even been outside London. 'It's beautiful here.'

Silvio drove along the coast road and Jessie leaned her head back against the seat, enjoying the feel of the sun on her face. Each sharp switch in the road took them higher, until the sparkling sea was far beneath them, the dramatic cliffs falling away in an almost vertical drop. And he drove like a native, urging the growling sports car around hairpin bends in what appeared to be a breathless duel with death. Torn between fear and exhilaration, Jessie found herself praying that there were no cars coming in the other direction.

'Where are we going?' *Over the cliff?*

'I want to show you something.' A pair of sunglasses obscured the expression in his eyes as he turned onto a narrow dusty road and parked by an old abandoned monastery. Wildflowers clustered in the long grass and a bright green lizard clung to a rock, basking in the hot sun. 'We have to walk from here. The streets are too narrow for modern transport.'

Jessie released her seat belt, her eyes on the lizard. 'What did they use as transport when they built the place?'

'Donkeys.'

Jessie smiled, finding it surprisingly easy to imagine a docile donkey plodding through this sleepy village. 'It's very pretty. And quiet.'

'A large proportion of the population have moved away.' Silvio took her hand and led her through a maze of streets, stopping in front of an old house. The shutters were closed, the paintwork was tired and it was obvious that no one lived there.

Sensing that it had some significance, Jessie looked at him. 'Is this what you wanted to show me?'

'I was born in this house.'

'You lived here? In this little village?' Jessie realised she'd never given any thought to where he'd lived the first years of his life, but perhaps that was because her own horizons had been so limited. She sensed that bringing her here was a huge thing for him and she was desperate not to say the wrong thing. 'When did you move away? You never told me anything about your early childhood. Johnny told me your father was violent—' She broke off, wishing she hadn't mentioned that, but he scooped her face into his hands and kissed her gently.

'There is nothing you cannot say to me, *tesoro*,' he said huskily, his mouth lingering on hers. 'Nothing.'

For a man who was so incredibly private, it was a huge concession and Jessie felt a slow, delicious warmth spread through her body. He trusted her. 'Is your father still alive?'

'No.' His voice hardened and he released her reluctantly, stepping towards the house. 'I came back here for the first time three years ago. I had a diary of my mother's and I traced some of the people who had known her.' He stretched out his hand and rubbed his fingers along the fractured paintwork.

'You came back after Johnny died?'

'Yes.' Silvio glanced up at the windows on the upper floors. 'I didn't want to be in London any more.'

'Because of me.' Jessie felt a stab of guilt. She'd sent him away. 'I—I'm sorry.'

'You have nothing to be sorry for. I played a huge part in Johnny's death.'

'That isn't true—you did try and help, I see that now.' Feeling hideously guilty, Jessie wrapped her arms round herself, shivering despite the sunshine. 'I was wrong. I was wrong about so many things.'

His eyes on her face, Silvio drew her firmly into his arms. 'You have forgiven me?'

'When Johnny died I was devastated—I blamed you because it was easier than blaming myself.' Jessie faced the truth for the first time. 'I felt as though I'd let him down. I was angry. It seemed like such a waste. I kept thinking that if I hadn't gone to work that day, if you hadn't given him the money—'

'You did everything that could have been done.' He was cool, measured—sure—and she wished she had even a fraction of his self-belief.

'Did I? I don't know.' Jessie leaned her head against his chest. 'I loved him and that stopped me seeing him how he really was. He was weak. When we were taken into care, he was so bitter and angry—I was only five, but he was fifteen. He'd known another life and he resented the fact that he'd lost it.'

'You'd lost it, too.'

'I was so much younger. And maybe that isn't an excuse. Should your childhood dictate who you become? Or is it a matter of personal choice?'

He stroked her hair gently, his touch both reassuring and soothing. 'It's probably not as straightforward as that.'

'Isn't it? Your background was worse than ours. Our mother was an alcoholic and she wouldn't have won any awards as best parent, but I think she did her best. Your father was violent. You were brought up with violence. Most people would have carried on down that path. But you left it behind. You chose not to be that person any more. Why? How could you do that when Johnny couldn't?'

'Each person is different. And I agree that the past shouldn't dictate the future. No matter what life you live, we all have choices.'

And he'd made the right choices.

Jessie lifted her head and looked at him. 'Can you forgive me for blaming you?'

He kissed her gently. 'There is nothing to forgive. It's behind us, *tesoro*. I want you to forget it.'

Jessie wasn't convinced, but she decided not to pursue it.

They'd already spent too much of their relationship talking about Johnny. 'It's hard to believe you once lived here. How old were you when you left Sicily? Do you remember it?'

'I was ten. And, yes, I remember it.' He moved away from her then, looking up at the house that had been his home. Standing there, he looked every inch Sicilian. Despite the external trappings of wealth, no one would have questioned his origins. He belonged in this wild, beautiful country—his glossy black hair and bronzed skin affirming his Mediterranean heritage. 'I remember how afraid my mother was as she smuggled me onto the ferry in the middle of the night. And I remember getting ready to defend her from my father if he followed us.'

Shocked, Jessie tried to imagine how it must have felt to be forced to protect your mother from your father. 'And did he?'

'I don't know. My mother had planned an intricate escape route—I doubt he would have caught us even if he'd tried.'

'You must have been very angry with him.'

'Yes, although it turned out that living with him had taught me two very useful skills—how to fight and how to keep myself emotionally detached. Both came in very handy when I found myself in a foreign country unable to speak the language.' Silvio took her hand and led her further up the street into a shaft of sunlight. Above them the sky was a pure, perfect blue without a cloud in sight. It was almost impossible to believe that such a beautiful place could hold such bad memories for him.

'It must have been awful to leave a country that was your home and go somewhere strange.'

'My mother picked London because she had a relative there, but there was no Sicilian community. We lived in a tiny flat on the border between two rival gangs. And there was I—

ten years old, speaking no English, dark skin. You can imagine.' He gave a wry smile. 'I was a perfect target.'

Jessie had a vision of how he must have been then—a small boy with olive skin, eyes the colour of black thunder and a temper to match. Angry with his father. Angry with the world. 'I can imagine who came off worse. You must have surprised them.'

'Yes, I think it came as a bit of a shock. I fought so fiercely that from then on everyone wanted to be on my side.'

'I can't imagine why,' Jessie said dryly, watching as two stray cats approached them hopefully. They were thin and hungry looking and somehow they made her think of Silvio. He'd been on his own on the streets, fighting for survival. Thinking how far he'd come filled her with awe. 'I don't know how you got yourself out of that situation. How did you even imagine that there was a different life out there?'

'My life acted as a catalyst.' Still holding her hand, he strolled back down the street towards the car, walking in the ribbon of shade created by the houses. 'I was fiercely determined to escape and create something different.'

Jessie thought of the yacht. The helicopter. The supercar. 'Well, you certainly got yourself something different. Do you ever find it difficult living this new life of yours?' She kept her voice casual. 'Do you ever feel out of place?'

'Never. If anything, I feel more at home in this life than I did in the other.' Confident and sure of himself, Silvio looked every inch the billionaire as he led her back to the Maserati. A crowd of children had gathered around it and Silvio spoke to them in Italian. They laughed and fell back, watching with envy as this sleek, successful man slid behind the wheel and started the engine.

As they left the village behind, Jessie stared out of the

window. 'You must have found it hard, coming back to rescue me,' she murmured. 'You thought you'd left all that behind.'

'I have left it behind.' The muscles of his forearm flexed as he shifted gears. 'It was just a fleeting visit.'

Jessie didn't understand why she found his words upsetting. He was rejecting that life, not her. But it was hard not to dissect every word he said and examine it in minute detail.

Wasn't she part of what he was so determined to leave behind?

Didn't she represent the life he'd turned his back on?

'Are you hungry?' He pulled up in a small fishing village and parked the car. 'I know a fantastic restaurant here.'

'Fantastic?' Fresh from her latest bombardment of insecurity, Jessie rubbed her hands over the pretty cotton skirt that she'd worn for the trip. 'I'm not really dressed for anywhere smart—I don't want to embarrass you…'

Silvio frowned sharply. 'I've already told you, you never embarrass me. And it isn't smart in the sense that you mean—it's the food that's incredible. All the locals eat here.'

The waiter showed them to a table right by the water and Jessie could see fish darting just under the surface, playing hide and seek among the rocks. The painted wooden chairs were simple and a surreptitious glance around her showed her that everyone else was casually dressed.

'There's no menu.' He lifted a jug and poured wine into her glass. 'You're given whatever the chef has prepared.'

And it was delicious. As Jessie savoured the best fish she'd ever tasted, she started to relax. Silvio talked about some of the big projects he was working on and she tried to look as though having a conversation about multi-million-pound developments was something she did every day, whilst in reality it was hard not to gape at him and say '*How* much?'

And all the time she was agonisingly conscious of every move he made, from the flick of his lean, bronzed fingers as he tore the bread to the flex of his shoulders as he reached across to put something on her plate.

He was breathtakingly handsome and unapologetically male, and she couldn't take her eyes off him.

Part of her was desperate to ask him what was going to happen once she'd sung at the wedding, but another part of her wasn't sure she wanted to hear the answer.

He enjoyed her company, she told herself, otherwise why would he be spending the day with her?

But she couldn't shake off the feeling that this felt more of a holiday romance than a proper relationship.

The novelty of being with her was going to wear off, wasn't it? He wanted to leave everything from his past behind…and that would eventually include her.

After a long, lazy lunch they strolled back to the Maserati and Silvio pulled her to his side as a moped popped and spluttered past them. Jessie saw a flash of long blonde hair and a seductive smile as the girl on the moped gave Silvio a lingering look, endangering life and limb in the process.

Jessie slid into the car, feeling invisible and ever so slightly sick.

Everywhere they went, women stared at him.

He could have been with anyone.

But he was with *her*, she reminded herself fiercely, hiding her expression behind a pair of oversized sunglasses.

She was making herself miserable for no reason.

Yes, he'd bought her a wardrobe, but she'd left her flat with nothing so that had been a necessity rather than an indication that she embarrassed him.

'You're very quiet.' Silvio slid into the driver's seat and looked at her with a frown. 'Is something wrong?'

If he wasn't noticing the differences between them, she wasn't going to draw attention to the problem. 'Just worried about singing at the wedding.'

'Why would you be worried? You have an astonishing talent.' A thoughtful look on his face, he stroked his fingers through her hair in a possessive gesture. 'When you sing tomorrow, everyone else will discover your talent. I predict that your life will change in a moment.'

'It's tomorrow?' Jessie felt a rush of trepidation. 'I hadn't realised that it was tomorrow. I haven't had a rehearsal.'

'We will arrive in the afternoon and you can rehearse with the band members.'

'I don't even know what they want me to sing. I might not know the songs.'

'They're happy for you to sing whatever you like.'

'What have you told them about me?'

Silvio smiled and started the engine. 'That they should make the most of your reasonable rates because after you've sung at their wedding, you'll be too expensive for most people to hire to sing at a private function.'

Jessie groaned, thinking of the expectations that people would have. *And how she was going to disappoint everyone.* 'You're living in fantasy land.'

'It's reality.' Silvio gripped the wheel with strong, confident hands. 'Wait and see.'

'It isn't reality! I'm not sure I can do it. Can't you ask someone else?'

'They want the best. And you're the best, Jessie.'

'I'm nobody, Silvio.' She stared straight forward as they drove back along the dusty roads towards the yacht. 'If this is the society wedding of the decade, they're going to want someone famous.'

'Trust me on this one, Jess.' There was a hint of exasperation in his smile. 'By the time you've finished the first song, you'll be famous.'

'Don't say that! Don't put so much pressure on me.' She ran her hand through her hair and winced because it was stiff from the wind and the salt. 'You just don't get it, do you? I can't stand up there in front of all those rich people and sing.'

'You sing all the time, Jess. You were always singing. It doesn't matter who you're singing to. It certainly doesn't matter what their income is.'

'Yes, it does. They'll all be judging me.'

'They'll be envying you,' he said dryly. 'As anyone would when they hear a talent like yours. You're happy to stand in an alleyway and fight off a bunch of thugs, but you won't sing in front of people who have wealth. What sort of logic is that?'

'Warped, probably,' Jessie admitted, 'but it's how I feel.'

'You'll be fine.' He parked the car and turned to face her. 'You just need to forget the audience. I'll sit in the back. You can sing for me.'

Realising that she couldn't make him understand, Jessie dropped the subject. He was confident in this new world he inhabited. He'd earned his place among the rich and famous.

She stared at the yacht—a visible symbol of his astonishing achievements.

It had been slightly easier to forget the differences between them when they'd been driving round the island. She'd felt like a tourist. Lovers on holiday. Today she'd spent time with the man, not the boy she'd once known.

Looking at the boat, it was hard not to feel like an impostor, but still she relished the new closeness that had sprung up between them.

He'd said that she could ask him anything, and she found it remarkably easy to do so.

In the intimacy that followed another incredible love-making session, she lifted her hand and touched his scar. 'In all the years I've known you, you've never told me about this. There were so many rumours but you never talked about it.'

Silvio was very still. 'It was a long time ago.'

'Sorry, I shouldn't have asked.'

'I told you, you can ask me anything.' He slid his hand behind her neck and lowered his mouth to hers. 'I'm not proud of that time. I'm not proud of who I was.'

'You chose a different life. You should be proud of that.' Jessie remembered the night in the alleyway. 'And the scar has its uses. It helps scare people away.'

But he didn't laugh. Instead, he rolled her onto her back, his dark eyes oddly intense as he gazed down at her.

'Do I scare you?'

'No.' She lifted her head and pressed her lips against the scar. 'You never scare me.' The thought of losing him scared her, but she wasn't going to admit that. She had no idea what was happening between them—what any of it meant. What would happen when she'd sung at the wedding? He'd said he'd give her a job, but would that be somewhere far away from him?

Feeling the cold fog of loneliness seep towards her again, Jessie tightened her grip on his neck and he frowned sharply.

'Tell me what you're thinking.'

'Nothing.' She could hardly tell him that she didn't want this to end, could she? 'I'm still worrying about singing at the wedding.'

'I don't ever want you to be scared.' His tone savage, Silvio lowered his head and took her mouth. 'You're mine now. You shouldn't be frightened of anything.'

Jessie wound her arms around his neck. 'No one has ever made me feel the way you make me feel.'

He smiled, supremely self-confident as he kissed her. 'How do I make you feel?'

'Special,' she said huskily, and then grinned. 'And sexy.'

'You are sexy,' he groaned, sliding his hand down her thigh. 'Too sexy for your own good and my self-control. I've never wanted a woman the way I want you. It's very unsettling to be this out of control—you have no idea.'

'I'm glad.' Feeling ridiculously powerful, Jessie nibbled at his lips. 'I feel the same way.' She snuggled closer, thinking that when they were like this, everything seemed right. 'Tell me about your scar.'

He stroked her hair gently. 'It was a turning point for me. There was a teacher at school—'

'I didn't know you ever turned up at school.'

'I occasionally honoured them with my presence,' he said dryly. 'This guy taught metalwork, and in his spare time he did property development. He offered me the chance to earn money so at the weekends I used to go and work on his building sites. I loved the feeling of building something instead of knocking it down or spraying paint over it. The night I received this...' he angled his head so that the scar was clearly visible '...I was working for him. A rival gang came and tried to wreck the building. I knew they'd make it look as though it was me and I was determined that wasn't going to happen.'

'So you fought.'

'Fortunately he'd installed CCTV so there was video evidence that I was acting in self-defence. No one touched me again. The teacher gave me a loan. I started doing my own thing and I discovered that success is more addictive than any of the substances sold on the streets.'

'Are you still in touch with the teacher?'

'Yes. He runs a community project that I sponsor.'

He sponsored a community project. He helped disadvantaged kids like he had been. He might have left it behind but he was taking plenty of people with him into his new life.

Jessie stared into the darkness, thinking about what Stacey had said about him helping people. 'I remember the night Johnny brought you back to our care home.'

'He'd strayed into the wrong part of town.'

'And you rescued him.' Thinking of that time hurt so much she could hardly breathe. 'You were always rescuing him.'

'He didn't want to be rescued. It was Johnny who made me realise we all had a choice.' Silvio tightened his hold on her. 'Johnny hadn't been brought up in that culture. I couldn't imagine anyone choosing the life I was living.'

'He was angry with the world. I was very young when we lost the life we had, but I remember him being angry. And then he was suddenly hanging around with the wrong crowd and he thought it was cool. Tough.' She took a deep breath. 'I suppose it gave him the chance to express all the anger he felt. He never believed he could change anything. You saw a different path, but he only saw the one he was standing on.'

'Can I ask you something?'

'Of course.'

His hand cupped her face. 'What's in the shoebox, *tesoro*? It was the only thing you brought from the flat.'

'It was the only thing I cared about.' Without hesitating, Jessie slid out of the bed and retrieved the shoebox. Silvio had shared secrets with her, hadn't he? 'It's all I have left of him.' Sadness flowed through her and she sat on the edge of the bed and removed the lid. A lump in her throat, she lifted out a photograph. 'This is my favourite. It's of the three of us.'

'I remember that day.' Silvio propped himself up on one elbow and reached for the photo. 'We came to your school to watch you play netball.'

'And almost caused a riot.' Jessie smiled through her tears.

'I was the most popular girl in the school after that day. Everyone wanted an introduction to my bad big brother and his equally bad friend.'

Silvio reached across and took the rest of the photographs from her. 'I remember this one too—you came second in that talent competition.'

'And Johnny swore at the judges because he said I should have come first.' Jessie sighed. 'I kept these pictures because they're all I have of him.' Remembering too late what else was in the box, she tried to close it but he was faster than her.

'You kept it?' His voice husky with emotion, the cheap locket dangling between his fingers. 'I gave you this on your sixteenth birthday.'

She didn't tell him that she'd worn it every day until that terrible night.

She didn't want him to know how much it had meant to her. *How much her adolescent brain had read into the gift.*

'It's very pretty.' Noncommittal, Jessie took it from him and put it back in the box along with the precious photographs and her ancient stuffed rabbit. 'Part of my past.'

'And what about your future?' Silvio leaned back against the pillows, watching her. 'What do you see?'

Her heart rate doubled. She was seeing a future where they were together, but she knew that wasn't going to happen. Silvio wasn't a man who settled down, was he?

'At the moment I can't see further than singing at this wedding tomorrow.' Keeping her tone casual, she put the lid back on the box. 'I see me opening my mouth and no sound coming out. I see guests trying to look polite but secretly wondering where on earth you dragged me from.'

Silvio pulled her back down on the bed and covered her mouth with his. 'Stop it,' he murmured against her lips. 'Now, I want you to close your eyes and visualise a different scenario. In this one, you open your mouth, you sing and everyone is silent. They stop talking, they stop laughing, they stop gossiping about the bride, because no one has ever heard a voice like yours.'

Jessie squeezed her eyes shut and giggled. 'No. It's no good. That's not what I'm seeing.'

'Then look harder,' he advised silkily, stroking his hand over her thigh and moving over her. 'What can you see now?'

Paradise, Jessie thought blindly as she felt his mouth on hers.

She could see paradise, with dark clouds gathering in the distance.

They arrived at the hotel the following morning, and Jessie felt sicker and sicker as Silvio guided her through the lush, beautifully tended gardens towards the main entrance. The cool, linear architecture seemed to blend with the landscape and the long curve of private beach was just a few paces away from the main hotel building.

Jessie felt as though she'd been deposited in the middle of a film set.

'The building took two years to complete but we were named Top Spa in Europe this year,' Silvio told her as he pointed out the luxurious treatment rooms that overlooked the sea. 'I've arranged for you to be pampered this afternoon. You need to have your hair and make-up done so that you look your best.'

So that she didn't embarrass him? Jessie gave a quick smile. 'Thank you,' she said politely, telling herself that it wasn't unreasonable of him to want her to look good—he'd arranged for her to have this job. This was an important, high-profile wedding. Of course he wanted her to be a success. 'And I'd like to rehearse at some point.'

'I've arranged that too.'

As they walked through the sliding glass doors into the luxurious marble foyer, the staff were almost embarrassingly deferential. Jessie shrank backwards but Silvio clamped his hand over her wrist and drew her against his side.

'Stop hiding,' he murmured, and then turned his attention back to the manager, who was hovering at a discreet distance, anxious to talk to him. After a brief exchange in Italian, Silvio gave a frown and turned to Jessie with an apologetic smile. 'I'm really sorry, but I need to abandon you for a short time to deal with some issues. Romana will show you to our suite and then take you down to the spa. You can spend the afternoon being spoiled and then I'll introduce you to the band. You'll have plenty of time to rehearse before this evening.'

'That sounds perfect.' Her smile stiff, Jessie followed the immaculately groomed girl through an archway and into a set of rooms that epitomised cool, modern luxury. The suite was uncluttered and light, and beyond the open doors was a private terrace with a small infinity pool that appeared to blend seamlessly with the sea.

'Someone will bring your luggage and unpack for you,' Romana told her, 'so I will show you to the spa.'

'You speak very good English.'

'Silvio insists that all his staff speak some English. He sends everyone on a language course when they first come to work with him.'

With him.

Not *for* him. *With* him. 'Have you worked with him for long?'

'Since this hotel opened. He is a very good boss, I think. This is the spa…' Romana led her through another archway and Jessie was completely captivated. A cooling breeze came off the sea and the blues and greens of the water were reflected in the calming decor of the spa.

'It's beautiful.'

'We're very proud of it.' Romana introduced her to a woman wearing a crisp white uniform. 'This is Viola. She will be in charge of your treatments. If there is anything at all you need, just ask her.'

Jessie followed Viola to a treatment room overlooking a private stretch of beach and proceeded to spend the next few hours in a state of pampered bliss.

She was massaged with scented oils, given a manicure and a pedicure and then guided through to the hotel's exclusive salon where an expert stylist shaped her hair and applied her make-up.

Stunned by the change in her appearance, Jessie stared at her reflection in the mirror and wondered if all those glamorous women who had attended the champagne reception spent this long getting ready every day.

It was a full-time job, she thought, being beautiful.

It was hours later that she finally made her way back to the suite. The band members had been friendly and talented, but the nerves were a tight knot in her stomach and she knew she wasn't singing as well as she could. She expected to find Silvio pacing impatiently, wondering how long it took for one woman to get ready to sing a few songs.

Instead, she saw two boxes on the bed, together with a note.

Curious, she opened the note first, frowning as she read:

To give you courage. S.

Wondering what he could possibly have bought her that would give her courage, Jessie opened the first box, delved through layers of fine tissue paper and gasped.

It was a gold dress.

But this was nothing like the cheap version she'd had to mend so many times. It was a work of art. Exquisite and unique.

Almost afraid to touch it, Jessie wiped her fingers on her towelling robe to make sure they were clean and lifted it carefully from the box. It flowed over her fingers like a liquid, the fabric so fine that it draped lovingly over everything it touched.

It shimmered and gleamed in the evening sunlight and Jessie quickly stripped off her dressing gown and stepped into the dress. It dipped low over her breasts, curved in at the waist and pooled on the floor in a river of gold.

'I knew it would look fantastic on you.' Silvio's hands were at her back, sliding up the zip, and she gave a soft gasp and turned to face him.

'You chose this for me?'

'I thought if you were wearing gold, you could imagine you were back in the bar.' He gave a faint smile. 'Not that I would have thought you wanted to be there, but you didn't appear nervous when you sang there.'

'It's really weird,' she confessed in a soft voice, her fingers sliding into the lapels of his dinner jacket. 'Whenever I sang there I pretended I was somewhere else—somewhere like this. And now that I'm here, I'm so nervous I'll have to pretend I'm back there.'

'Once you start singing, you'll be fine.'

Jessie looked down at herself. 'The dress is truly stunning. It wasn't one of the ones I tried on, was it?'

'I had it made for you. Everything you touch will be gold once people have heard you sing.'

Jessie tried to dismiss the thought that he hadn't trusted her to choose her own dress for the evening—that he'd been afraid she might make a fashion faux pas.

Cross with herself for even thinking that, she reached for the other gift. 'What's this?'

'No more battered cardboard boxes,' Silvio said softly, sliding his hands over her shoulders and watching while she opened it.

Jessie removed the packaging and revealed a box the same size and dimensions as hers—only this one was gold, inlaid with an intricate pattern, and she knew instantly that was extremely valuable.

'Open it,' Silvio urged, and she did so cautiously, wondering why she felt so numb.

Was he afraid that one of his staff might come across her battered cardboard box?

But if the box had surprised her it was nothing compared to the contents. Inside was a glittering diamond pendant on a bed of scarlet silk. Nestled in a setting of gold, it was a more expensive replica of the one he'd bought her years before and Jessie stood in stunned silence as he fastened it round her neck.

'Time to throw the cheap version away,' he purred, standing back and looking at her with a satisfied expression. 'It looks good on you.'

'Silvio, I can't wear this!' Her voice barely a whisper, Jessie touched it with the tips of her fingers.

'I might lose it. Or someone might mug me—'

'The hotel is swarming with security staff. And anyway...' he gave a faint smile '...if someone tries to mug you, you can stab them with your shoe. Or you could just punch them. We both know you're more capable of defending yourself than any of the other women out there.'

Her hand still on the diamond, Jessie gave a choked laugh. 'I don't think that sort of behaviour goes with the dress.'

'Fine. Leave it to the security staff, then. Or me. I'll be watching. Are you ready?'

Jessie looked in the mirror. On the outside she looked every bit as glamorous as any of the women who had attended the champagne reception on his yacht.

On the inside, she felt no different.

She was like a sturdy family car that had been re-sprayed and fitted with a Ferrari engine.

She was a fake.

She wanted to say something about how she felt but she knew that anything she said would sound ungrateful. And she wasn't ungrateful. Far from it. She just wished she didn't feel as though he was…she swallowed…*upgrading her*?

Silvio held out his arm. 'Are you ready?'

'Now?' Her eyes widened and panic gripped her. 'I need more practice.'

'You don't need more practice.'

'Aren't they eating dinner or something?'

'They're just finishing their second course. They're ready for music. The other musicians said you were fabulous.'

'I wasn't fabulous, actually,' Jessie said honestly, suddenly overwhelmed by nerves. 'I didn't sing well. And they were just normal people.' Her mouth was so dry she couldn't imagine being able to sing a note. 'Why am I doing this? I'll let you down. You haven't heard me sing since I was a child.'

'I've heard you sing, Jessie.' Clearly unable to understand her panic, he smiled. 'I was in Joe's bar a few nights ago. It took a great deal of will power not to drag you from that stage, I can assure you.'

She stood still while the words sank in. 'You were there? I didn't know.'

'Well, tonight you will know.' Dismissing her fears, he lifted her hand to his lips and kissed it. 'And when you sing, you will be singing for me.'

Her insecurities melted away.

He cared for her.

He'd bought her the gifts because he was generous and he wanted her to feel confident, and she was being stupid and paranoid. He wasn't upgrading her—he was spoiling her.

'Thank you,' Jessie said softly, smiling up at him. 'Thank you for everything you've done for me. Shall we go?'

Silvio sat at the back of the room, watching Jessie walk onto the stage.

The laughter and chat didn't cease and most of the guests didn't even notice that she'd joined the other musicians.

The bride and groom were drawing all the attention, as was to be expected, because this had been the most antici- pated wedding for a decade and everyone who was anyone had been silently hoping for an invitation.

As the pianist started to play and the rest of the musicians joined in, no one broke off their conversation or even looked in their direction.

And perhaps that was just as well, Silvio thought wryly, watching Jessie's hand shaking as she reached for the micro- phone. If she thought they weren't looking, she might find the courage to open her mouth.

The diamond pendant he'd given her glittered at her throat and the dress dipped seductively, while still managing to be discreet. Even though it was subtle and understated it was every bit as sexy as her tight gold dress.

Given that no one was taking any notice of her, Silvio was severely tempted to haul her off the stage and take her back to bed. He had to remind himself that this was her big opportu- nity.

This was her dream.

He lifted his glass and drank, trying to ignore the nagging

voice that told him he'd taken advantage of her desperate situation.

Their relationship had nothing to do with the fact that he'd rescued her. Nothing to do with the gifts he'd showered on her.

He'd acted on the chemistry that had always been there.

She'd chosen to start with a love song, slightly jazzy, nothing too intrusive. Silvio saw her glance nervously at the pianist, and then as the opening notes of the piano faded Jessie started to sing and he gave a slow, satisfied smile, sat back in his chair and waited.

Her voice slid over the room like a spell, silencing conversation and stilling all movement. Waiters stopped serving, even her fellow band members stumbled over a few notes, too busy gaping at her to concentrate on what they were doing. But Jessie didn't stumble. She sang as she always sang, her beautiful voice so unbelievably perfect that no one listening could have doubted that she was a star.

As she hit the top notes, the hairs on the back of his neck stood up and Silvio wondered how she'd managed to spend so long in obscurity with a voice like hers.

But he knew the answer to that.

Sometimes you needed life to give you a break.

And he'd given her that break.

Silvio glanced sideways, noticing that the women on the table nearest to him had tears on their cheeks.

No one was eating. No one was talking.

When Jessie finished the song, no one moved and he saw her look at him with panic in her eyes and launch straight into the next song.

He held her eyes, listening to the words of love that flowed from her lips and her heart, understanding that she didn't have the courage to look at anyone else.

The words were soulful and intimate—far more intimate, he realised, than anything they'd said to each other in the privacy of the bedroom.

The fact that she was so unsure of herself sent a flicker of exasperation through him.

How could you have a voice that held everyone in thrall, and not be sure of yourself?

Silvio ignored the food on his plate and the champagne in his glass. He was as captivated by her voice as the rest of the people in the room. And then the song ended. There was an explosion of applause and everyone was on their feet.

He saw the shock on her face. Saw her look from him to the audience, disbelief and excitement lighting her eyes.

And he knew that Jessie had got her break.

Just as he'd predicted, her life had changed in an instant.

Jessie felt as though she was floating on air.

Not just because of the amazing response of the audience but because she'd seen the pride glowing in Silvio's eyes and as she'd sung to him she'd realised that she'd meant every word.

She was in love with him.

She'd been in love with him all her life.

And he had feelings for her too, she knew he did.

Why else would he have done so much for her?

Why else would he have given her the gold dress and the pendant?

As Jessie sipped the champagne someone had handed her, the compliments bathed her in a warm glow. It was like living your life in winter and then suddenly discovering summer.

She was desperate to share her feelings with Silvio, but she couldn't fight her way through the throng of people keen to talk to her.

Cameras were flashing in her face and she gave an interview before she even knew she was talking to a journalist. Hoping they weren't going to print anything embarrassing, Jessie turned to find a tall man with grey hair waiting to talk to her.

'So has Silvio arranged a recording deal for you?' The man drew her to one side and Jessie took advantage of the space to take a breath.

'No.' Baffled by the question, she looked at him. 'Why would he?'

'Because Silvio Brianza has an unerring eye for a good investment and you must be one of the best investments he's ever unearthed. The guy is a genius, I have to hand it to him. I don't suppose I can persuade you to desert him and fly with me to Las Vegas, can I?' Delving into his pocket he withdrew a card. 'My daughter is getting married next week. I'd love you to sing. Who is your agent?'

'I—'

'Contact him. Tell him I'll pay a million dollars for the evening.'

Jessie almost fainted. 'A million dollars? You have to be joking.'

He frowned. 'I've insulted you. I apologise. Would you consider doing it for two million? I'm impressed that you know your worth.' He moved to one side as someone elbowed him. 'I realise you're in demand, but I hope I hear from you.' With a nod and a smile he walked away and Jessie flopped onto the nearest chair, feeling as though she was going to pass out.

Had someone really just offered her two million dollars to sing for an evening?

Feeling light-headed, she automatically looked across the room, searching for Silvio so that she could tell him the news and they could laugh at it together, but she could no longer see him, so instead she sat for a moment, trying to catch her breath.

'Silvio really does know how to spring surprises.' A beautiful woman sat down next to her and lifted glass of champagne in a silent toast. 'Have you known him long? Or are you another one of his sob stories from the gutter?'

Jessie felt her mouth dry. 'Sob stories?'

'Yes, you know…' The woman suppressed a yawn. 'All those people he rescues. He'd rescue the whole world if he could. It's quite sweet really, Silvio's soft streak. He dragged himself from the streets and he likes to help others if he can. I don't blame him. These days it's good business to have a social conscience.'

Jessie felt her happiness shatter. 'Silvio doesn't care about his image. He helps people because he wants to make a difference.'

'Well, he's certainly succeeded with you. Although does it really work, I wonder? This type of social engineering.' The woman put her glass carefully on the table and rested her perfectly manicured hand on the linen tablecloth. 'It seems a bit cruel to me. Do you honestly feel part of this crowd?'

Jessie felt as though her face was frozen. It was impossible to move any of her muscles. 'I'm fine.' Fine. She was the one using that word now.

'Oh, you look the part. He's done a good job on your appearance, but are you happy? Or are you just looking round comparing yourself to everyone else?'

Jessie felt numb. She'd thought she was happy.

She'd thought this was the happiest day of her life.

'I'm not one of his good deeds. That isn't what this is about.' But it was impossible not to think about the gold dress and a diamond pendant. And the box. He'd replaced her battered old box with something special that would last for ever.

Why?

Jessie rubbed her fingers over her forehead, trying to ignore the voice in her head that was telling her that he was wiping out everything of her old life.

Her companion gave a sympathetic smile. 'If I've offended you, I'm sorry. I was just worried about you sitting here by yourself, not knowing anyone.' She sounded genuinely contrite. 'Why is Silvio helping you, then?'

Jessie couldn't formulate a response.

She tried to silence the nagging voice in her head that told her that if he'd cared about her as a person, it shouldn't have mattered whether she was wearing her cheap gold dress or his couture version. It should be about *her*, not about the clothes she was wearing or her ability to blend into his new life.

But he'd never talked about a future, had he? Never talked about love.

Silvio Brianza didn't fall in love.

Yes, he'd wanted her. But only after he'd dressed her up and transformed her into someone different.

Suddenly needing some sort of evidence that she was wrong, Jessie looked around for him again and this time spotted him through the crowd, deep in conversation with a stunning brunette. He appeared to be enjoying her company, a smile playing around his firm mouth as the girl flirted with him.

Watching the girl flick her hair and gaze at Silvio from under her eyelashes, Jessie felt the last dreg of hope ooze out of her.

She was deluding herself if she ever thought she could compete with that.

'That's Angelica De Santos, the Spanish actress. Silvio's

had an on-off relationship with her for years. They were together in Cannes earlier in the year. She's determined to be the one to pin him down, and perhaps she'll succeed. He certainly likes her. They're always being photographed together.' The woman next to her stood up, taking her glass with her. 'Good luck with the singing.'

Jessie didn't even hear her.

She was staring at the elegant, confident, poised woman who was still laughing with Silvio. Watching them, it wasn't hard to believe they'd had a close relationship. And why not? Both of them were single. Both of them were rich and glamorous. They were perfect together.

Silvio had never had to buy that woman a dress or show her what to wear. He'd never had to find subtle ways of disposing of an embarrassing box.

He'd never had to rescue her from an alleyway.

Jessie gulped down several mouthfuls of champagne, forcing herself to face the truth.

She *was* one of his projects.

Silvio had helped her because he felt guilty about Johnny, not because there was anything special between them. And how could there be? He was a billionaire.

And who was she? Not a supermodel or an actress. Just a girl from the back streets of London who happened to have a decent voice.

In the past few days she'd seen enough of the way that Silvio lived his life to know that he enjoyed the lifestyle that went with immense wealth and privilege. He'd moved on. And he had no intention of ever going back.

Even now he was too absorbed by his beautiful companion to bother coming over to congratulate her.

She'd accepted his help because she was desperate, but she wasn't desperate any more, was she?

She had no excuse to stay.

Far too proud to be a burden on anyone, Jessie stood up quickly and searched the crowd for the man with the grey hair.

She had no idea where Las Vegas was, but she knew it was a long way from London. And a long way from Sicily. It sounded like a good place to start her new life.

And two million dollars would mean she could repay Silvio everything she owed.

No more debts to be paid. No more blame.

Nothing.

It was over.

From across the room Silvio watched with growing tension as Jessie talked to the most influential figure in the music business. It took all his self-control not to shoulder his way through the crowd and drag her away from the man who was, without doubt, trying to sign her to his record label.

'Silvio! You've cut yourself!' Angelica broke off flirting with him and took a step backwards. 'The stem of your glass has broken—how did that happen?'

He'd made it happen, he realised blankly, staring down at the razor-sharp glass and the blood on his fingers. 'Weak glass.'

'Or strong fingers,' Angelica said dryly. 'Don't you dare get that on my dress.' She removed the glass carefully from his hand, placed it on the tray of a passing waitress and helped herself to a napkin. 'Use the napkin, Silvio—you might be perfectly comfortable with blood, but the rest of us have weaker stomachs. Then tell me what's made you so angry.'

'I'm not angry.' Silvio took the napkin from her and pressed it to his finger, his eyes still focused on Jessie.

She was surrounded by people congratulating her.

And she wasn't even looking in his direction.

Angelica peered through the crowd. 'Oh—I see. Brad is interested in your little protégée—you must be pleased.' She looked up at him and her beautiful eyes narrowed. 'You're not pleased.'

'Of course I am,' Silvio said, his tone neutral. 'A music career has always been her dream.' And he had plans to arrange it for her—plans of his own.

He watched as Jessie listened attentively to what Brad had to say.

He thought of what they'd shared over the past week—

The fact that she'd given herself to him and no other man.

The breath hissed through his teeth as he watched Brad hand her a business card.

She wouldn't go with him, would she? This man she didn't know—this stranger who was probably offering her the world…

Any moment now she was going to turn and look at him. Then she'd walk across to him with that excited look in her eyes and tell him about it—*ask his advice*—

Angelica sighed. 'You're lousy company, Silvio. If I didn't know you so well, I'd be offended.'

'*Mi dispiace.* I'm sorry.' Silvio tore his gaze from Jessie and looked at the beautiful woman by his side, barely seeing her. 'What did you say?'

'Nothing important.' Angelica gave him a meaningful look. 'If you feel like that about her, why haven't you already got your ring on her finger? You're not usually slow to grab what you want.'

'It isn't about what I want.'

Anglelica's eyes widened. 'Then you really have finally fallen in love,' she drawled, 'because up until now it's only ever been about what you want.'

Love?

Was this how love felt?

Frozen with shock, Silvio didn't respond. Instead, he turned his head to look at Jessie again, only to find that she'd gone.

He scanned the crowd, trying to spot her.

But there was no sign of her.

Angelica sighed. 'I feel invisible. Go after her, Silvio,' she said wearily. 'What are you waiting for?'

What was he waiting for?

A stranger to doubt and prevarication, Silvio was asking himself the same question.

He was well aware that he'd given Jessie a taste of a life-style beyond her wildest dreams. He was also aware that he hadn't given her a choice in any of it. He'd dragged her away from the alleyway, he'd refused to let her return to her flat, he'd bought her a new wardrobe—a new life…

And he'd made love to her.

When she had been feeling at her most insecure and vulnerable, he'd introduced her to a whole new world of intimacy.

Acutely aware that his behaviour had fallen far short of perfect, Silvio ran his hand over the back of his neck and swore in Italian.

'I speak Italian,' Angelica said, her eyes amused. 'Just go after her, Silvio!'

'I'm not going after her,' he said harshly, letting his hand drop to his side. Jessie felt obligated to him, didn't she? She was always thanking him, clearly embarrassed that he'd given her so much even though it meant nothing to him in financial terms. He knew how proud she was. If she hadn't been desperate, she never would have come with him. 'If she wants to stay, that has to be her decision and her decision alone.'

But would she?

He'd given her the opportunity he'd promised her.

And suddenly Silvio realised that he'd done more than show her a new life.

He'd made it possible for her to leave him.

CHAPTER NINE

'FIVE minutes, Miss Gray.' There was a rap on her dressing-room door and Jessie checked her reflection in the mirror, feeling as though she was looking at a stranger.

Where was the bedraggled, terrified woman Silvio had rescued from the alleyway only two months earlier?

Her make-up had been professionally applied, her dark hair fell in perfectly arranged curls and her dress was the work of Hollywood's favourite designer.

The man with the grey hair who had made her such an extravagant offer had turned out to own a record label. Within days of arriving in Las Vegas and singing at his daughter's wedding, rumours about Jessie's voice had spread and every night she found herself singing to an enraptured audience of thousands.

And at the end of every performance she was returned to the luxurious penthouse suite that had become her temporary home. Anything she wanted was just a phone call away.

Jessie stared at herself in the mirror. *Not quite anything.*

She'd disciplined herself not to allow her thoughts to wander in that direction, so she stood up quickly, reminding herself that she was living her dream.

Someone from the publicity department had left a stack

of newspapers and magazines on her table, all featuring articles about her.

Had Silvio seen any of them? When he saw her name in a newspaper did he read it with interest or did he fling it to one side and turn his attention back to some gorgeous blonde?

Did he think of her at all?

Obviously not, or he would have followed her.

She'd left the wedding in Sicily without speaking to him but she had written him a note, thanking him for everything that he'd done for her. And she'd heard nothing from him. Since then she'd sent him a cheque, repaying everything she owed him. And still she'd heard nothing.

The fact that he hadn't even contacted her to see how she was getting on was devastating. It simply proved how little he cared for her, Jessie thought miserably, nodding to the stage manager, who was waiting.

Clearly Silvio considered that he'd fulfilled his obligation to her.

This particular project of his had been successfully concluded.

As Jessie walked onto the stage, she heard the roar of the crowd and felt the familiar flutter of nerves in her stomach. Even after weeks of performing here, she still felt nervous but she'd developed a routine to calm herself. She touched her pendant briefly, stared into the darkness of the auditorium and imagined that Silvio was out there somewhere, listening to her.

And when she started to sing, she forgot everything except the song itself.

She sang as she always had, the only difference being that this time when she sang of love and loss, she was singing from experience. And even though she was facing the audience that had once featured in her dreams, she still closed her eyes. This time she was remembering a curve of perfect white sand and the dizzying smile of a very imperfect man who was all she'd ever wanted.

The song ended, she opened her eyes and for a brief, breathless moment she thought she saw his face in the crowd.

Wishful thinking, she told herself, acknowledging the applause with a gracious smile. Despite the fact that the audience was on its feet and she could see people near the stage crying, she didn't feel as happy as she should.

Feeling frighteningly empty, Jessie launched into the next song and then the next, keeping the audience sweetened with her honeyed voice, trying not to think about those magical few days in Sicily.

Her performance ended and she accepted the applause, the cheers and the flowers with grace and then took the private lift back to the penthouse.

Locking the door, Jessie slid her shoes off and walked barefoot across the expensive rug.

'Why are you living on the top floor?' The male voice came from a chair by the window and Jessie jumped with shock.

'Silvio—?'

'You hate the top floor.'

He was here? 'You almost gave me a heart attack.' She pressed her hand to her chest, feeling her heart bumping crazily. 'What—? H-how did you get in here? The door was locked.'

'There are some advantages to a misspent youth.' Silvio rose to his feet and strolled over to her. 'You haven't answered my question. Why the top floor? You can't sleep if you're on the top floor. Who put you up here?'

The fact that he knew her so well somehow intensified the dull ache in her chest. 'This is what they gave me and I didn't like to say anything,' she murmured, still unable to believe that he was actually here.

'So every night you sleep right by the fire escape, is that right?'

Her eyes met his and she didn't bother lying. 'Yes.'

He scowled angrily. 'You should have demanded something on the first floor.'

'I'm not the sort of person who demands anything. And anyway, if I'd done that they would have wanted to know why and I hate everyone knowing personal details about me. Every day the press write another story—it feels weird, like having a shower and then realising that you've left the doors and windows open and everyone can see you naked.' Having him so close made it hard to breathe. An image of his dangerously handsome face was permanently lodged in her brain but her memory had somehow dimmed reality. Or perhaps she had been subconsciously trying to make him something less. Less handsome, less strong—not someone worth breaking her heart over.

But the man standing in front of her radiated raw power and confidence and he was looking at her in a way she found hard to interpret. 'So how are you finding your new life? Is it everything you wanted?'

'It's fantastic,' she lied. 'Wonderful to have been given so many opportunities. I'm loving it, obviously.'

His gaze was impassive. 'So why do you have black rings under your eyes?'

'I'm tired. Singing here and then commuting to California to record the album—it's hard work—and sleeping next to the fire escape isn't that restful.'

Conscious of how close he was, Jessie took a step backwards because the desire to touch him was almost too much to bear. 'Can I get you a drink or something?'

They were making polite conversation, stepping around each other.

'No, thank you.'

Flustered, confused and appalled by the strength of her own feelings, Jessie licked her lips. 'Why are you here, Silvio?'

'I'm checking on you,' he said softly. 'Last time we parted, I didn't check on you. You wanted me out of your life, so that's what I did. I left your life. And not once in those three years did I find out how you were. I haven't forgiven myself for that.'

'I'm not your responsibility.'

His jaw hardened. 'If I'd kept a closer eye on you I would have found out how much trouble you were in. And it never would have escalated the way it did.'

'I didn't want you to check on me. If you'd turned up, I would have sent you away. Why are you bringing this up now? It's all in the past.'

'Yes.' His eyes didn't shift from hers. 'It is. And I'm going to make sure that it's not repeated in the future.'

She had to remind herself that his protective instincts were triggered by guilt and nothing more. 'So you're saying that you're going to look me up every now and then to see if I've managed to get myself into trouble? You don't have to do that, Silvio. You've already done more than enough for me. It's because of you that I have this opportunity. But if that's why you're here, to make sure I'm okay, then you've done it. Here I am.' Jessie spread her hands and gave a casual shrug. 'I'm in one piece and flourishing. So now your job is done. When are you planning to check on me next? I'd like to know so that I can prepare myself for another heart attack when I discover an intruder in my home.'

Silvio stared at her for a long moment and then turned and

paced over to the window, his movements restless and impatient. 'Why didn't you tell me you were coming here? Why leave a note? That night in Sicily—could you not at least have told me in person that you wanted to go?'

She hadn't wanted to go.

'I couldn't get near you for glamorous actresses,' she said lightly. 'And anyway, this is what you wanted me to do, isn't it? You wanted me to sing. As one of your projects, I've turned out pretty well. You can congratulate yourself and go back to your flashy life with a clear conscience.'

He turned to look at her, his expression impossible to read. 'Is that what you think you are? A project? A salve to my guilty conscience?'

Her heart lurched. 'Isn't that what I am?'

'You obviously haven't heard the rumours. I don't have a conscience, Jess.'

Jessie lifted her hand and slowly removed her earrings. 'You rescued me from the streets—literally—when my life was in a mess. That night in the alleyway, when I realised it was you, I was relieved and horrified at the same time. I felt safe and I felt threatened. I'd never been so confused about anything.' She put the earring down on the table. 'Then you showered me with clothing and gifts, flew me to your yacht and introduced me to a life that I hadn't even known existed. Why would you do all that if it wasn't because you felt guilty?'

'That's an interesting theory, but it has one major flaw.' The phone in his pocket buzzed and he slid his hand into his jacket and silenced it instantly. 'Where does sex fit into that little scenario?'

Jessie felt her face heat and opened her mouth to respond but nothing came out.

'I'm extremely selective who I take to my bed,' Silvio

drawled, a dangerous gleam in his eyes. 'First, the woman in question has to be sexually attractive, but she also has to have a certain level of courage and independence before I'm going to be interested. I'm not good with limp wallflowers. And I've never, ever made love to a woman out of guilt.'

Her mouth was so dry she could hardly speak and her heart was hammering so loudly that she wasn't sure she'd be able to hear his response. 'Angelica looked as though she fits your criteria.'

Silvio stood perfectly still, not making a move to approach her. 'Before I answer that, I want to know why you left that night. What did he offer you? Why did you leave without even talking to me?'

She lifted her chin. 'Why did you let me leave?'

Something flared in his eyes. 'Because I was a fool,' he breathed, 'and I made a mistake. Another one of many mistakes I have made with you.' He strode over to her but Jessie took several steps backwards.

'You were with Angelica—she was flirting with you.'

He frowned impatiently. 'Angelica doesn't know any other way of communicating with a man and don't tell me she's the reason you left because I won't believe you.'

'What is it you want, Silvio?' she whispered, and he lifted an eyebrow.

'You really have to ask me that? I've crossed a continent to find you and I'm sure you know that chasing women across the globe is not generally a habit I indulge in.' A sardonic smile touched his firm mouth. 'Just for the record, I've never had to chase a woman before. Not even over a short distance.'

'So why—?'

'Doesn't that tell you why I'm here?' His voice shimmered with exasperation and tension was visible in every line of his handsome face. 'I want you, *tesoro*. And no other woman.'

Her heart turned a somersault in her chest. 'That isn't true.'

'You know it's true. I've always wanted you. From the day of your sixteenth birthday when I gave you that locket. I could hardly keep my hands off you even then, but everything collapsed around us and I knew it could never work,' he said thickly, taking her face in his hands and forcing her to look at him. 'And then I saw you in that alleyway—being away from you for three years hadn't changed a thing.'

Jessie felt dizzy. 'You didn't tell me how you felt.'

'Talking about emotions is as alien to me as analysing them,' Silvio confessed in a raw tone. 'And anyway, I didn't know how I felt until I thought I'd lost you. Look at me, Jessie.'

Her heart pounding, she looked. 'Silvio—'

'I want you to look at me and see who I really am.' His tone savage, he released her and stepped back. 'I want you to remember where I came from. I'm not some clean-living, well educated boy from a good family. This face of mine is a constant reminder of the life I led.'

'I know what your life was, Silvio.'

'Do you? Or have you forgotten? Perhaps you see the yacht and the helicopter—the man who can buy anything he wants.' His voice was tinged with bitterness. 'But I was bred into a life of violence and you have no idea how difficult it has been to leave all that behind. It's the reason I work so hard. I can never relax. I never feel far enough away from it. I've been running since I was a teenager, and I'm still running. I will *not* go back there.'

'Why are you telling me this when I know it already?' She spoke in a whisper, stunned by the passion she saw in him.

'I was there with you. I lived that life. I know where you came from. You don't have to explain it for me. Why are you saying these things to me?'

'Perhaps I'm delivering a warning.' His mouth twisted into a smile of pure self-mockery. 'You talk about guilt, Jess, and, yes I feel guilt. I want you, but I know you deserve better.'

'Better?' Jessie laughed, hope blossoming in her chest. 'Does it get any better than this, Silvio?'

He inhaled deeply, his expression strangely uncertain. 'I'm not the man for an innocent girl.'

'Am I supposed to be the innocent girl in this scenario? I'm twenty-two, which makes me a woman, not a girl, and if you think I'm innocent, perhaps you don't know me as well as you think you do.'

'You were a virgin, Jess.'

'Yes.' This time she didn't deny it. 'And the reason I was still a virgin is because you're the only man I've ever wanted. I was never interested in anyone else. Even when I thought I hated you, I still didn't want anyone else.'

Some of his tension eased but there was still doubt in his eyes. 'Is that true?'

'You know it's true. You have always known how I felt about you.'

Silvio lifted his hand and touched her cheek gently. 'I hurt you. You were vulnerable and inexperienced and I hurt you.'

'It was the most incredible experience of my life.'

'Then why did you leave?' He cupped her face in his hands, his tone demanding. 'The night of the wedding—you just walked away from me. Why?'

'Because I thought it was the right thing to do. Because I thought I wasn't good enough for your new life, because I was afraid that being with me reminded you of the life you'd left behind…'

'I wanted the future to be your choice,' he said roughly. 'I wanted you to choose me—us—not because you felt indebted to me but because that was the life you wanted.'

Her eyes filled with tears. 'I didn't know I had that choice,' Jessie whispered, her voice cracking. 'I didn't know there was an "us" to choose, Silvio.'

'You knew how I felt about you.'

'No.' Jessie shook her head. 'I didn't. I thought I embarrassed you.'

'You have never embarrassed me.'

'You kept dressing me up.'

He exhaled slowly. 'I was spoiling you—you've had such a hard life. I wanted to make you happy. And I knew you felt self-conscious so I thought the clothes would help.'

'I thought that every time you looked at me you remembered the life you'd left behind. You kept trying to turn me into something else.'

He gave a disbelieving laugh. 'I bought you gifts because that was the only way I knew to show you how much I cared.'

Jessie hesitated. 'I thought perhaps… Y-you weren't trying to upgrade me?'

Muttering something in Italian, Silvio hauled her into his arms. 'I would never want to upgrade you—you're the only model I want.'

Happiness flooded through her like sunshine on a summer's day, warming all the chilled corners of her heart. 'If you really do want me, that's all I need to hear.' She felt the muscles on his shoulders tense under her fingers and he leaned his forehead against hers.

'You're sure? I'm not pretending you're the first woman

I've been with, Jessie—and I'm not pretending I've ever been any good at relationships.'

'Then it's time you changed your ways,' she said calmly, the love she felt for him bubbling up inside her. 'You didn't need to say any of this to me, Silvio. I grew up in the same place you did. I always knew who you were. I knew where you came from. And I knew what I wanted. I always did.'

'And what do you want?' His voice hoarse, he tilted her face to his with a firm hand. 'Now that you're here with the world at your fingertips, what is it that you want?'

'You,' she said shyly, her body heating as she felt him hard against her. 'I want you.'

His mouth came down on hers and he kissed her long and thoroughly. 'I'm never leaving you again,' he groaned, sliding his fingers into her hair and holding her face still as he covered her with kisses. 'And you're never going to leave me. If there's somewhere you need to sing, I'll go with you. You're getting far too much attention and I need to make sure everyone knows you're mine.'

Unable to believe her good fortune, Jessie was instantly anxious. 'Why do people need to know I'm yours? Are you sure there isn't something else going on? Is this still about those thugs?'

'My sources tell me the thugs are in custody.' His touch was both protective and possessive. 'They won't bother you any more. And this has nothing to do with them.'

'Then…'

'I love you, Jess.' He said the words fiercely, his eyes burning as he looked down at her. 'And the best way to show the world you're mine is to put my ring on your finger. So you're going to marry me.'

Everything stood still and she stared at him in silence.

Silvio drew in a breath that was decidedly unsteady. 'That

came out all wrong,' he confessed unsteadily. 'I really messed it up. I meant to ask you, not tell you. I wanted to be romantic. Can you pretend you didn't hear? I'll try again.'

Jessie burst out laughing. 'Silvio…'

'I've never told a woman I love her before—and I've never proposed.' Uncharacteristically unsure of himself, he ran his hand through his hair. 'It isn't as easy as it sounds.'

'Silvio, I—'

'Don't refuse me without giving me another chance,' he said hoarsely, taking her hand to his lips and kissing it in an old-fashioned gesture. 'I love you, *tesoro*. Will you marry me? If you agree to take a risk and marry me, I promise you won't ever regret it.'

There was a lump in her throat. 'I'm quite good at taking risks.'

'I'd noticed.' There was a dangerous gleam in his eyes and he tightened his grip on her hand. 'So are you willing to take a risk this time, or are you standing there wondering why you'd be stupid enough to marry a guy with a background as unstable as mine?'

'You're seriously asking me to marry you? Not just live with you?'

'I want it all, Jess. If you don't know that about me, perhaps you don't know me as well as you think you do. I want everything I can have with you.'

'I can't believe you feel this way about me. If you were letting me choose, and you thought I'd chosen this life, why did you follow me?'

He gave a sheepish smile. 'You didn't make the right decision.'

'So I can choose, as long as I make the choice you want me to make?' Jessie shook her head, her eyes brimming with laughter and tears. 'You need serious work, Silvio Brianza.'

'*Sì*, I do,' he said urgently, 'and it is going to take you decades to finish that work. So the sooner you get started, the better. Is the answer yes?'

She lifted her hand to his cheek, overwhelmed by the love she saw in his eyes. 'I assumed you let me go because you'd finished with me.'

'I hadn't even started, *tesoro*.' He pulled something out of his pocket and Jessie felt him slip something onto her finger. 'I forgot this, didn't I? Remind me never, ever to propose to a woman again.'

'Don't worry, I won't let you,' Jessie assured him, feeling slightly faint as she looked at the enormous jewel sparkling on her finger.

'This is the beginning of our life together. The public are in love with their new star, but you are mine first. You were always mine. This ring tells the world you're mine.'

So happy that she felt light-headed, Jessie wrapped her arms around his neck. 'It's stunning—but you have to stop buying me things.'

'That might be a problem,' Silvio confessed, pulling her gently towards the chair he'd been sitting on. 'I'm addicted to buying you things. And I have something else that I think you might like.' He bent down and picked up a small package.

'What have you bought me this time?' Jessie ripped off the paper and pulled out a camera. 'Oh—Silvio!'

'You need something with which to record the memories that you treasure so much,' he drawled softly. 'In thirty years' time you can give the photos to our grandchildren.'

Overwhelmed by the thought as much as the gift, Jessie took it from him and stowed it safely in her gold box, which went everywhere with her. Inside were all her old photographs, her ancient stuffed rabbit and another photograph that she hadn't seen before. It was a photograph of *her*.

She lifted it out, her hand shaking. 'Did you put this there? When was this taken?'

'Your eighteenth birthday.'

'I've never seen it.'

'That's because I kept it.'

'You kept a photograph of me?'

'*Sì*, but please don't tell anyone or next time we are threatened in a dark alleyway they will be laughing, not retreating,' Silvio said dryly, prising the box out of her grip and putting it down on the chair. 'And now I want you to stop looking at memories and create some new ones with me instead.'

Choked with happiness, Jessie flung her arms around his neck. 'I don't want to go back to London. I want to live on the yacht and sail to different places. I want to take photographs of everywhere we go.'

'What about your singing career?'

'I'll sing if it fits in with what we're doing.'

'We can live on the yacht if that is what you want.' His tone indulgent, Silvio smoothed her curls away from her face. 'And when you have my babies and we are nervous parents, I will build you a villa in Sicily near our favourite beach.'

'Babies?' It was something she'd never allowed herself to imagine.

'Of course—we cannot have grandchildren without first having children. That's the way it works, *tesoro*.' Amusement shimmering in his dark eyes, he lowered his head to kiss her. 'I am a Sicilian man. I want a family. A proper family who will stick together and support each other. And you will be an exceptional mother. If they inherit your vocal skills, we will have our own choir. It will make us a fortune.'

Laughing, Jessie rolled her eyes. 'Does everything have to be a commercial opportunity? Even our children?'

He gave an unapologetic shrug. 'That is who I am, you know that.'

'Yes, I know.'

'Then you will also know that I love you. *Ti amo.*' Silvio lowered his head and Jessie lifted her mouth to his with a blissful sigh.

millsandboon.co.uk Community

Join Us!

The Community is the perfect place to meet and chat to kindred spirits who love books and reading as much as you do, but it's also the place to:

- **Get the inside scoop from authors about their latest books**
- **Learn how to write a romance book with advice from our editors**
- **Help us to continue publishing the best in women's fiction**
- **Share your thoughts on the books we publish**
- **Befriend other users**

Forums: Interact with each other as well as authors, editors and a whole host of other users worldwide.

Blogs: Every registered community member has their own blog to tell the world what they're up to and what's on their mind.

Book Challenge: We're aiming to read 5,000 books and have joined forces with The Reading Agency in our inaugural Book Challenge.

Profile Page: Showcase yourself and keep a record of your recent community activity.

Social Networking: We've added buttons at the end of every post to share via digg, Facebook, Google, Yahoo, technorati and de.licio.us.

www.millsandboon.co.uk

2 FREE*BOOKS
AND A SURPRISE GIFT

We would like to take this opportunity to thank you for reading this Mills & Boon® book by offering you the chance to take TWO more specially selected books from the Modern™ series absolutely FREE! We're also making this offer to introduce you to the benefits of the Mills & Boon® Book Club™—

- **FREE home delivery**
- **FREE gifts and competitions**
- **FREE monthly Newsletter**
- **Exclusive Mills & Boon Book Club offers**
- **Books available before they're in the shops**

Accepting these FREE books and gift places you under no obligation to buy, you may cancel at any time, even after receiving your free books. Simply complete your details below and return the entire page to the address below. You don't even need a stamp!

YES Please send me 2 free Modern books and a surprise gift. I understand that unless you hear from me, I will receive 4 superb new books every month for just £3.19 each, postage and packing free. I am under no obligation to purchase any books and may cancel my subscription at any time. The free books and gift will be mine to keep in any case.

Ms/Mrs/Miss/Mr_____ Initials _____

Surname _____

Address _____

_____

_____ Postcode _____

Send this whole page to: Mills & Boon Book Club, Free Book Offer, FREEPOST NAT 10298, Richmond, TW9 1BR